HOLIDAY IN HELL

Also by Jan Huckins

With Irma Phillips
Lonely Women
As "Sebastian Blayne"
Terror in the Night
With Carolyn Weston
Face of My Assassin

HOLIDAY IN HELL

SEBASTIAN BLAYNE

CUTTING EDGE

Published by
Cutting Edge Publishing
PO Box 8212
Calabasas, CA 91372
www.cuttingedgebooks.com

This book was previously published under the title "Gay Ghastly Holiday"

To know the worst leaves no dread more.

...

It sets the fright at liberty
And terror's free—
Gay, ghastly holiday!
—Emily Dickinson

CHAPTER ONE

How will it happen? Moira thought. What will it be like the next time? I am waiting. I pretend I'm not, but every moment I am waiting for it. The silent turn of the oiled lock, the muffled step, the approach of an alien body in the dark, breath held in. I know he is there but I cannot scream. Why do I think of a man? Could those hands that searched for me have been a woman's hands? But I am safe here in Malibu. There is peace in the sand and the sun. Sleep. Lie on the beach and rest, Max said, but I can't. There is always part of me watching, awake, on guard. Then feign sleep. No one knows where you are, who you are. You are Mr. and Mrs. Hadley from New York, who have rented a beach house for the winter.

But she continued to listen and watch. The wind rippling the white fringe of the blue umbrella, the surf beating on the shore, and Max's even breathing were the only sounds she could hear. Clasping her knees and shaking with cold in the brilliant sunshine, the woman looked around warily, scanning the beach. Not a child, not a dog, not a fisherman, not even a boat on the horizon. Stretched beside her on the sand was the body of a man whom she knew as Max, whom she resented now because he could sleep. It had been months since she had slept an undrugged hour—all the months of nights since the police had found Ida Gibbons with a knife in her back.

Moira shivered convulsively, remembering the sweet sickly smell at the morgue, and suddenly she understood. It was here too, the smell of death, poisoning the clean salt air.

I have brought it with me, she thought, I cannot escape it. Sebastian Blayne cannot protect me, Max's love cannot save me. I have wondered before, perhaps I am strange, perhaps I do dream things that aren't real, but I didn't imagine the hands around my throat or the man that time in the garage. They were meant to be warnings. Now the ending is close. I couldn't explain why I know, but I know. It will be here in this place.

"Darling." Max opened his eyes and smiled lazily. "I haven't been asleep. I've been watching you."

She made no answer, waiting for him to ask the inevitable question.

"What were you thinking about?"

"You always ask me that."

"Because you never tell me."

His eyes, she thought, were like the ocean, changing with the light from Mediterranean blue to turquoise to green. "It wasn't important, Max, really. Nothing in particular." Before he could say anything else she leaned over and kissed his upside-down face.

Suddenly he sat up on one elbow. "Moira, you've got no clothes on."

"I want to tan evenly."

"It isn't decent."

"No one can see us."

He relaxed and lay down again. "Do you like having a private beach?"

"Naturally." She lit a cigarette and put it between his lips. "I like everything you give me."

"Everything?" He laughed. "I'm surprised we're speaking this morning."

"Why?"

"Well, after last night …"

"Oh, that." She dismissed the subject with a flick of a finger-nail. "What would be the point in not speaking? We never say anything."

He frowned. "Still mad? I hate it when we fight."

"So do I. What was it about?" She knew well enough. "Too many Scotches, I imagine." Moira answered herself too quickly. It suddenly seemed very important to keep Max in a good humor. She reached for his hand and placed it on her breast.

Last night had been a mistake, but she had been exhausted by the urgency of their escape and the fear of being followed, trembling with fatigue after the long plane trip, the mysterious drive in the dark from the airport to the unknown house at the beach. Long after midnight, when Max had finally locked their rented car in the garage, they had sat in the musty, overly ornate living room, drinking and arguing.

The house Max had leased sight unseen as Mr. Hadley (a thousand-dollar deposit down and no questions) was a two-story early Roman DeMille-type villa painted coral pink with a white roof, situated on a lonely stretch of beach along the shore road. This road was seldom traveled in the winter, when most of the beach houses were vacant. A high wall lined by cypress trees separated their garden from the outside world; there was only the sea in front of them and they had no neighbors. So there might be a chance still to be safe here, evade the pursuer, shut him out.

"We don't need to use the upstairs at all," she said. "All those little halls and twisting stairs. One could fall so easily." And there are too many rooms, too many dark corners where a man might conceal himself.

"What are you talking about?" He opened his eyes again.

"Our pink *palazzo*."

"Never mind that. What was wrong with you last night?"

"Only tired," she said.

"Not tired of me?"

"No, Max."

"They why did you run away from me?"

Could she ever explain to him how this nameless, faceless fear had devoured her?

"Why? Without telling me? You weren't afraid of *me*?" The sun had gone under a cloud; his eyes were opaque, a deep cobalt.

"I wasn't myself."

"That goddamn interfering Blayne bastard."

"He was trying to help me."

"Help you out of my life. You weren't coming back." He made it a flat statement, not a question or an accusation.

"I didn't make any plans. I just wanted time to think."

His hands, long familiar with her body, slipped possessively down her thighs and drew her to him. "Now I've got you back, Moira, I'll never let you go."

His kisses began to excite her and she pulled his head down to her breast. "Baby. You're my baby," she said, and saw that it might be true. He needed her more than she needed him.

"Do you know how long it's been?" he whispered. "You were in the hospital and then—"

"Don't talk," she gasped softly.

Now he will be happy, she told herself. I belong to him again. From the first time I saw him it was like this. I didn't know him, I didn't care who he was. When he kissed me, that was it. I gave myself to him that night and ever since. Yes, yes, yes, yes. He knows I want him like this. But I don't love him any more, that died somewhere along the way. Oh, God, if I could only get away without making him angry, without his suspecting....

But even while she was trying to escape in her mind she died at his touch, whispering his name, whispering, "Max, Max, Max," without a sound, forming the words with her mouth pressed against his hair while he kissed her breast, biting her until she cried out in pain and passion. Still he held himself away from her, cruelly teasing. Of the sadistic stallion and the masochistic mare, who is to say which is victor and which vanquished? The sun climbed to its noonday zenith, the arching sky was cloudless, and they lay a long time.

"You'll never leave me again, will you?" he begged.

Even at the moment that she promised passionately to stay with him (and some part of her did mean it), Moira was considering the possibility of getting in touch with Blayne. But fearing Max might read her mind (he could sometimes), she buried the thought under a great many words and little kisses.

Later in the afternoon they went for a walk along the beach and were talking about something else entirely, when he asked out of a seemingly clear sky, "Blayne knows where you are?"

"No, darling. How could he?"

"I thought you might have written him."

"No." She turned from him to stand at the water's edge and let the foam of a little expiring wave lick at her toes, watched it recede, imagined its long journey back to the South Seas, to China, to the other side of the world, where no one had ever heard of Moira Ryan.

"Do you really like it here?" Max sat down at her feet where the waves had been. "You wouldn't rather go somewhere else?"

Anywhere! a voice screamed. Anywhere to escape it. In one quick movement she sat down cross-legged beside him and with a shell drew their initials, two entwined M's with a straggling heart around the letters. "No, darling," she said.

"I'm glad," he said, and squeezed her hand hard, apparently satisfied. "We can have a real holiday first." He began to dig a tunnel. "Have fun."

"Fun," she repeated absently. "What do you mean, first?"

"Before anything else happens."

Their eyes met and his were cold gray now. Did they change with the day, with the weather, or with his mood? "What else could happen?" she asked, scooping up a handful of sand and letting it slip through her fingers.

"I was thinking of all the mess we've left behind us. My brother—"

"But it is behind us. We'll begin again."

"Do you think we can?" He too sifted the sand in a fine stream, staring at the falling grains as if they could reveal the mystery of time itself.

"If you hadn't convinced me of that, I wouldn't be here."

"Sure we can, baby, sure."

She insisted, "That's what you said in Chicago."

"I thought it was the only way out—for us to be alone and get away from things." With a stick of driftwood he leveled the sand from his tunnel. "Moira baby," he said, "will you always remember I love you?"

"I remember everything." She watched the doodle he was drawing. "I even remember the way we used to be."

"How was that?"

"Oh, so many things. You used to call me honey-bug."

"Did I? Sounds terrible."

"I liked it. What's that on top of your tunnel?"

"That's no tunnel, it's a driveway into the garage. Then you walk upstairs into the living room." He drew a square. "Our bedroom." Then a smaller square. "And this is the kid's room."

She caught her breath before she laughed. "It must be the sun."

"Of course we'll have him. Why not?"

"Ronnie live with us?"

"Didn't I say it?" He put his lips on her sun-warmed skin and nuzzled the back of her neck, kissing the fine little hair that grew there. "I don't like your hair brown. Will you let it grow back?"

"You know why I did it."

His fingers touched the short ringlets. "You don't look like you. I could imagine you're someone else."

"I'd be jealous," she said, and built a terrace onto their house, a barbecue pit, a rumpus room (for what parties, what friends?), and a kitchen. "Would you like it if I were someone else?"

"No, you wouldn't be you."

"Sometimes I wish we'd just met and you weren't rich, and we had no"—she hesitated—"no pasts."

"Everyone has a past. If I didn't have mine and you didn't have yours, we wouldn't be here." Again he ran his fingers through the short-cropped curls, stopping at the scar. "Whoever did that to you, I'm going to kill him when I find him."

She got to her feet and brushed off his suit. "You promised, Max."

He stood up and faced her. "All right, I won't talk about it. But haven't you any idea at all?"

"I've told you and told you—I don't know."

"You're positive of that?"

"Yes. I'm positive."

"There's no one you suspect, even remotely?"

"No." Once more she was able to meet his eyes. "There's no one." She held her gaze steady. "Why?"

He didn't answer.

"Why do you think I'm lying?"

"Is there anything you've kept from me?"

She shook her head.

"Anything you haven't told me?"

"You know it all, Max." Then she went on quickly, "Please. I don't want to think about it anymore."

They must have walked a mile down the beach. On the way back Moira noticed that the tide was coming in. Their house had been washed away.

If she called Sebastian Blayne long-distance, would he refuse to help her? "I know I let you down, Neddy, but don't walk out on me now. This is the last thing I'll ever ask you ...." Remembering their first encounter on the telephone (how many months ago, how many lifetimes?), she wondered if he would make a rude noise and hang up in her face as he had in the beginning.

❧ ❧ ❧

On that January morning which Sebastian Blayne was never to forget, he had been awakened by a long persistent ringing. Outraged, he squinted at his Cartier clock. A quarter to nine. Who could be ringing him at this indecent hour of the morning? Who would dare?

"Beppo!" he yelled, but there was no answer. His plump little valet didn't arrive until ten. The phone continued to buzz softly, insistently. There were three phones on Mr. Blayne's right bed-side table—his private line, the hotel phone, and a direct wire to his publisher's office. One buzzed, one rang, and the other had a sort of death rattle. But Sebastian Blayne could never remember which was which. That was what Maggie was for. But his secretary was not due until noon. There was no escape.

On his second try, he was able to stop the buzzing by removing the instrument from the hook. He had no intention of answering the thing. He made a raspberry noise and hung up. After a blissful moment the phone rang again.

"Mr. Blayne," a woman's voice kept saying. "Mr. Blayne." A pillow would solve that difficulty. But it was a rather nice voice, husky and yet somehow—automatically he searched for the exact word—silken. Blayne's elephantine memory began to stir; he was reminded of his third wife, and his curiosity, which was also monumental, prodded him into full consciousness.

"Madam," enunciated Mr. Blayne in his most Edwardian manner, "do you realize that you have robbed a weary man of the only solace that remains to him? I refer, of course, to the process of knitting up the raveled sleave. I was asleep."

"I'm so sorry." The nice voice did sound sorry. "I do hope you'll forgive the intrusion, but—"

"No excuses will avail you." No longer young, Sebastian Blayne enjoyed playing the eccentric. There were very few things left that he did enjoy. He had had all the money and all the fame and all the women.

"I read an article about you in 'Reader's Digest'—"

"Reprinted from 'Life.' That one?"

"Yes. I was very much impressed."

"Doubtless. That piece was autobiographical, ma'am. You should consult the 'New Yorker' profile on me. The comparison with Alexander Woollcott is libelous."

"But you *are* a detective?"

Mr. Blayne had certain rigid principles about dialogue over the telephone. After all, a noted dramatist cannot be too free with his repartee. "My dear young lady, would you mind stating your name and business? I suppose you have some excuse for disturbing me?"

"My name is Moira Ryan." She paused, seeming to wait for a reaction, but when none was forthcoming hurried on, "I thought perhaps you might see me for a few moments—later in the day, of course."

"I'm afraid that's quite impossible. I'm busy, as my friend Matisse said recently, packing my bags for another world." Sebastian Blayne tucked the phone under his much-photographed chin, lit a cigarette, and settled back into his ten pillows. Actually he loved lengthy and involved telephone conversations and he had every intention of seeing the young woman, but he would not make it too easy for her.

"In this article you said you were interested in criminology, and I"—there was a brief hesitation—"I have a case that might appeal to you."

The brief hesitation holds great significance for a playwright—the wicked little pause that says the unsayable. "You have a case? It concerns you?"

"Well—" Again the almost nonexistent pause. "No, a friend of mine."

Ah, thought Sebastian Blayne, the hypothetical friend. And his elderly faun's ears pricked up. "What's troubling your friend?"

"I can't explain over the phone."

"By the way, which of my phones are you on—if you don't mind a preposition?"

"That depends on the proposition," she said coldly.

"You're not sitting on my revered publisher's lap?"

The husky voice had a beautiful laugh, like three little chimes. Not silver but brass, good brass. "Whatever gave you that idea? No."

"Very few people know my private number, so this must be the hotel phone."

"It is."

"I don't understand how you got through. I have announcement service *and* the switchboard has strict instructions never to ring me before eleven."

"I know that, Mr. Blayne, but I also know the boss."

"The boss?"

"I really can't go into that now. If you'll have a cocktail with—"

"I don't like bars."

"My apartment, then?"

"I don't go gadding about to strange apartments, either. I'm very sorry, but if you can't tell me what all this hanky-panky is about, I'm afraid I must disappoint you."

Again she pleaded, "Not over the phone."

Blayne could hear her breathing. He let the silence grow.

Then she spoke rapidly in an urgent whisper. "I can't, I think we're being listened to."

Indignantly Blayne sat up. "You mean someone is monitoring my calls?"

"No, *mine,* Mr. Blayne."

Again there was a long pause. If an eavesdropper were present, he was very silent, Blayne decided, just as he heard a faint click. Goose flesh rose on his arms. How long since I've had goose flesh? he asked himself delightedly. But had he heard a click or only imagined it?

Moira Ryan spoke fast. "This friend of mine believes that someone is trying to kill her."

"Good." Blayne snuggled back into his pillows. "Where shall I meet you?"

"Take the elevator to the twenty-sixth floor and change to the lift for the penthouse."

"The penthouse? *Here?* At the Park Carlton?"

"That's right, Mr. Blayne." She laughed lightly. "Interested?"

"Mrs. Ryan—that *is* the name, isn't it?—you have not only succeeded in arousing my interest, I am now morbidly curious."

"Shall we say five o'clock, then?"

"That should allow me sufficient time to pull myself together," he sighed. "The penthouse. At five. Oh, wait, Mrs. Ryan, one more thing. I like Martinis very dry and very cold. A jigger of Noilly-Prat, a drop of absinthe, a fifth of gin—and don't forget to rub garlic around the glass."

"That's not a Martini, that's murder."

"What am I saving myself for?" he asked sternly, and hung up. But he kept hearing her voice say, "murder."

When Beppo appeared, on the stroke of ten, tiptoeing in with black coffee, the morning papers, and a vase of red carnations, the master's bed was empty. From the bathroom issued a reedy wail. Beppo, through long experience, was able to distinguish the melody of *"La Fille aux cheveux de lin."*

Bland, round, bald-headed Beppo was the apple of Blayne's jaundiced eye. "He has charm, he is witty, he never bores me," Blayne liked to point out to his friends when they had the temerity to mention Beppo's less endearing characteristics. "What if he steals my books and brandy? Do I not benefit by his conversation derived from these very stimuli?" There was a deep understanding between Beppo and Sebastian Blayne; they had the same sense of humor, of play-acting, of creating an atmosphere of gaiety and ease. The servant was an antagonist worthy of Blayne's mettle—foe, friend, and foil.

Stretched out in the black marble tub full of blistering hot water, the writer contemplated his lean aging body. "No paunch," he said as Beppo entered. "No paunch yet."

Placing the vase of carnations on the toilet seat, the valet observed that his employer was in fine fettle.

"And how did you arrive at this conclusion?"

"I hear 'The Girl with the Flaxen Hair.' Therefore, I think we have met a blonde. No paunch—she must be attractive."

Beppo poured out two cups of strong black coffee, presented one to his master, and drank the other. "Would you like to start with the 'Times' or the 'Tribune'?"

The writer waved the newspapers away. "I understand there is a penthouse on top of this architectural monstrosity. Do you know who lives there?"

"The owner, Max Vienna."

"And who is Max Vienna?"

"He is the president of the Carlton hotel chain, comprising some fifteen or twenty hostelries of great prominence from here to yon." Beppo's gesture embraced America from the Statue of Liberty to the Golden Gate.

"Jewish, I take it?"

"No, he's Austrian, I believe, but not Jewish."

"That name—Vienna. Assumed?"

"Changed it legally from something unpronounceable. A fabulous success story. From peasant to penthouse in one generation. Are you looking for a plot?"

"No, a red herring," Blayne replied thoughtfully.

The matter continued to obsess Sebastian Blayne throughout his well-ordered day. Why should an unknown young woman invite him to a tête-à-tête in Max Vienna's penthouse apartment? During his sun-lamp treatment and rubdown Blayne decided that some skittish friend was playing a practical joke. He could not digest the 'Times' with his orange juice and eggs Benedict. When Maggie arrived he could not concentrate on his dictation. By lunchtime he was convinced that Moira Ryan's implication of foul play was nothing but dramatic license to ensure his appearance. "This dreadful girl has doubtless written a play she wants me to read," he confided to Beppo. His entire routine was shaken to the core.

Ordinarily Blayne's schedule of living and working was as rigorous and inflexible as royal protocol. On shipboard or the Superchief, visiting friends or basking on the Riviera, there had always been six hours out of every day dedicated to work, but recently his preoccupation with criminal behavior had begun to infringe more and more.

To his friends Blayne rationalized this indulgence: "A man of my age has few pleasures. The pursuit of literature is the only stimulant I take to excess. But to write, one must study man. The source material is all around one, good and evil. Lately I have become fascinated with the flowers of evil, shall we say? Yes, let us say that, for it is as good an excuse as any. It is not crime as such that attracts me, but the psychological motivations that engender violent and desperate actions. I know very little about guns, but in the course of my long and not uneventful career I have discovered a few things about the sort of person who uses a gun and what makes his finger pull the trigger. Ballistics is not my province, but as a dramatist I know how a poisoner thinks, and that applies also to the strangler, the butcher, and the more subtle murderer, the maker of accidents, the puppet master who manipulates the strings and causes someone else to kill for him. My friend Lieutenant Fennelley of the homicide squad is familiar with all the poisons known to science. He is an authority on lethal instruments, fingerprints, tire prints, laundry marks, tapped telephone wires, and dictaphone devices. His laboratory can restore burned documents so that the vanished print can be read. Simon can tell you what a corpse had for dinner, where he bought his clothes, and what taxi he took to his death. The Lieutenant, you see, thinks first of the victim, but I think primarily of his assailant. The murderer is my antagonist. It is a deadly game in which I have the advantage. He does not know me, but I have a picture of him. A cowardly man commits a cowardly crime; a daring man a daring crime. Remember that we always impute ourselves in our every dealing with others. The thief expects to be robbed, the trickster to be deceived. Everything we do or leave undone is a vital clue to our inner natures."

But Maggie, Blayne's redheaded secretary, was not deceived by her employer's psychological circumlocutions and refinements. "It's only boredom," she told Beppo, "but it could easily kill Neddy." The author was Neddy to his intimates, although he had long since dropped the Edward from his name.

On the morning of Moira Ryan's call Maggie found occasion to question Beppo privately. "What's upset him so?"

Beppo gave Maggie a brief résumé of the shocking facts. "Awakened betimes," murmured Beppo, who was currently deep in Pepys' Diary. "Missed his morning reading period, and you know what *that* does to him."

Maggie said, "Mm" vaguely. "Tell me about the woman."

"I haven't had time to investigate yet."

"Do you think we're headed for another wife?" Maggie, only five years in Blayne's employ, had lived through the last wife period. Beppo had seen three come and go; there had been four altogether. When Maggie had first taken up her secretarial duties (which term covered a multitude of extraordinary tasks), she and Beppo had begun as enemies, jealous of each other's domain and Neddy's affection. But Sheila, the fourth and last wife—the Irish setter bitch, as Beppo called her—had drawn the valet and secretary together for the sake of mutual protection. But theirs was an armed truce.

Beppo and Maggie were in the habit of pooling their information. She closed her eyes to the first editions that wandered from Blayne's shelves and never returned, the Courvoisier that evaporated, the suits that were lost at the cleaner's; and Beppo not infrequently sat up late at night copying manuscripts when Maggie's tumultuous love life interfered with the wheels of progress. Neither suspected that Neddy could distinguish his valet's typing from his secretary's, nor that he could count the number of bottles in a case.

"What's her name?" Maggie wanted to know.

"The hotel employees call her La Ryan."

"Not Irish again?"

"*Oui, ma petite.* But will you cast the first stone, Miss McMahon?" Maggie did not react, and Beppo continued, "I don't like it any more than you do. That last poison thing nearly wrecked his blood pressure—gadding around in a police car with Toots Shor and getting his feet wet. Besides, it's not dignified—his being shot at, I mean." Maggie nodded and poured herself a small Scotch. They were standing in the pantry. "I keep telling him—Ibsen was a recluse, G. B. S. stayed at home. And as you know all too well, we fully intend to take the dramatists' longevity championship away from Shaw."

"How's the new play coming?"

"Very spotty."

"Where did he go today?"

"Out in the park with Misty." Misty, or properly Mistinguett, was Blayne's elegant and temperamental French poodle of advanced years.

"Meeting anyone?" Beppo sat down on a red leather stool and folded his legs under him.

"He didn't say."

"I wonder what he's up to."

"We might take turns following him."

"Certainly," said Beppo. "It would be so easy. You could wear your invisible cloak and I could rent a flying saucer for aerial observation."

"Beppo, you slay me," said Maggie, but she wasn't laughing. "Someone has to protect him—from himself."

"Perhaps we're taking this too seriously."

"Too seriously? Don't be dull. You know Neddy. If he can't work, it's love or he smells a mystery. Either way it's hell on us. And we worry about him. He may look a jaunty fifty in a dim light, but actually he's a museum piece and much too important to go chasing after blondes."

"How do you know she's a blonde?" Beppo wanted to know.

"Aren't they always?"

"You're so right, Ma-gee. However, this one happens to be someone else's blonde."

"Huh?" Maggie reacted with sufficient violence to please even Beppo. That is to say, she put down her Scotch.

"It has come to me like a revelation, Margarita *mia*. Suddenly I am remembering a conversation with Fritz, the elevator boy. At the time I paid no attention to his backstairs gossip, but now, yes, it all comes back to me."

"Skip the establishing shot, dear, and get on with the narrative."

"Well, it seems that the big boss, Max Vienna, has a mistress he's nuts about, and jealous, but *green,* if anyone looks at her. Keeps her upstairs in the penthouse like a fairy-tale princess in a tower."

"To be rescued, a fairy-tale princess usually lets down her hair," Maggie murmured.

"I think she wants to with Neddy," said Beppo, and they held a council of war.

CHAPTER TWO

At one minute to five Sebastian Blayne rode the elevator to the twenty-sixth floor of the Park Carlton and there changed to the penthouse automatic lift, which took him one floor higher.

The foyer was a miracle of frosted glass, exotic plants, mirrors, and white marble table. Or perhaps there was only one table, Blayne thought as he rang the bell, feeling like Alice in Wonderland at the sight of his own image reflected from all sides. He was looking rather well, he decided, studying his Sulka tie, gray Homburg, and the blue suit that David Windsor had pronounced "not bad."

"Mistinguett, we make a charming couple, don't you think?" For reply the iron-gray poodle tried to squat in a tempting jardinere of giant rhododendrons. "You disapprove of the decor, my darling?" Mistinguett relieved herself quietly. "I agree with you. What taste!" One of the mirrors mysteriously unfolded and became a door. "Ah—Mrs. Ryan?" The Homburg came off.

"Hello, Mr. Blayne." She offered her hand. It was cold and small. "How good of you to come."

"Not at all. I expected at the least a footman in a powdered wig." He was chattering to help the nervousness he sensed in her. "Those mirrors in the foyer are—stunning."

"In the original sense of the word?"

He laughed and started to follow her down a long carpeted hall with more mirrors and chartreuse walls. "This is Mistinguett. Do you mind if she comes along?"

Moira Ryan frowned momentarily. "Not at all. Max doesn't like dogs, but he isn't here today, and I gave the servants the afternoon off."

Blayne admired her for the casual acknowledgment of her relationship with the millionaire hotelman as he watched her walking ahead of him to the glass-enclosed, radiant-heated terrace.

They were on top of the world, it seemed to Blayne. The view of Manhattan was stupendous. For a breath-taking moment he stared at the glittering towers, which were rosy pink in the late afternoon sun, towers with windows of beaten gold. There had never been a city, he thought, never a city in the world that could be compared with New York for glory and graft, beauty and badness.

"What are you thinking?" Mrs. Ryan asked, and handed him a Martini from the bamboo bar.

"Something literary." Blayne turned away from the view and helped himself to a ratan lounge chair. "Actually, I was wondering," he improvised, "how New York would look rising up into a mushroom-shaped cloud."

"I've never known a writer before," his hostess said respectfully.

"May I point out, Mrs. Ryan, that you do not know me. And secondly, that I am not a writer but a man of letters. There is a distinction."

"Is this a sample of your sardonic wit?"

"You've been reading about me," he accused.

"I haven't read a book for ten years, Mr. Blayne. Until someone told me you were staying here at the hotel I thought you were dead."

"So many people do. It used to annoy me. Now I consider it a great compliment. It's the same thing with Picasso. This is an excellent Martini."

"I merely followed your instructions. I've been trained to follow instructions."

A leading remark if I've ever heard one, Blayne thought, but he decided not to play up. She's made up her mind to tell me about herself, but she wants to be questioned. To ease her conscience, perhaps? Blayne's comprehensive eye took in Moira's features, cataloguing her costume in the filing cabinet of his mind. A hostess-coat kind of thing, long and flowing, flashing bright blue birds on a white background—by Jacques Fath? Star-sapphire and diamond clips, platform sandals, bare legs, a Miami suntan, frothy ash-blonde hair by Lizzie Arden, and a figure by— God? Honest eyes that matched the sapphires, a stubborn chin, but the mouth was pure passion. A contradictory and unpredictable kind of face. How old was she? Past thirty? She seemed no particular age; she was simply blonde and beautiful.

Blayne realized suddenly that the conversation had come to a complete standstill. "I've been talking and you haven't been listening," Moira Ryan said.

"I was thinking that you're really a rather staggering beauty."

"Staggering? On only one drink?" She got up and beckoned to him. "Come along, I want to show you something."

He followed her from the terrace through the living room to a small bar done in white leather, black mirrors, and chromium. "You have your own private night club," he said.

"It's a copy of a place where I used to work. You'll find the gin and vermouth on the shelf, ice cubes in the little refrigerator underneath." She sat down at the black-and-white striped piano and began to sing "Can't Help Loving That Man of Mine." Not a distinguished performer, but certainly professional, Blayne decided. She's got something, a style of her own. The husky voice had a sweet, sinuous quality.

When she finished, Blayne handed her a drink and a cigarette. "Moira, I am going to bestow a great favor on you. You may call me Neddy. I like your voice."

"Thank you. I haven't sung in ages. Max doesn't like me to sing for anyone." The capable hands with the long red nails hovered over the keys and started "Melancholy Baby" in a minor key. "Is it true that you solved the Marguery murders?"

"No, not exactly. I have a very shrewd and painstaking confrere on the police force, Simon Fennelley, who did all the real work. Why don't I ring him up and—"

She rose from the piano abruptly and crossed to the bar. "It's not a case for the police. My friend couldn't prove anything that's happened. Actually nothing *has* happened—except accidents."

"Then why is she frightened?"

"Did I say she was?" She measured the gin. "Will you have another?"

"Since neither my valet nor my secretary is here, I may. The truth is, I was born three Martinis below par. They help, as Montague once said, my mind rise to its natural stature. Now tell me about these accidents that haven't happened." There were two doors in the room, one from the hall and the other from the living room. He noticed that his hostess' eyes sought these two doors constantly, as if she were expecting someone to enter.

"Max told me he was going out of town on business, but I never know. He might walk in any moment."

"Then let's sit over here in the corner where we can watch both doors at once," Blayne said, as if it were the most natural remark in the world.

A pack of matches in the crystal ash tray was initialed M. V. In the center of the white leather bar the same letters occurred, done in mirrors. Mr. Vienna evidently liked his name and his face, Blayne decided. And then he remembered Moira's saying, "Max doesn't like dogs." Where was Misty? Snoozing on the terrace? "Max doesn't like me to sing for anyone." Did those two statements mean that there must be only one ego here? No other performer? Not a dog to be petted, or a singer who might steal the floor?

She sat down beside him on the banquette. "Mr. Blayne—"

But he stopped her and said, "Neddy," firmly.

She went suddenly arch on him. "I don't think I can call you Neddy. It's like calling Shakespeare Willie. But I'll try."

"Do try," he said, blushing for her. She was so utterly lovely and lost; why this unnatural coyness?

"A man like Shakespeare wouldn't have been easily shocked, would he?"

Blayne suddenly saw that she was making a literary pass.

"Tell me what it is I'm not to be shocked about."

"My offering you a retainer," she said softly.

He should not underestimate her, he warned himself, simply because she was clumsy. "A retainer—for this friend of yours?" He looked away to make it easier for her to lie.

"Yes. What sort of fee would you want?"

"Moira, I shall be quite blunt. I have too much money as it is. There's nothing you could offer me—" He was not prepared for her kiss but he let himself enjoy it. Deliberately leaning against him with her breasts, she put her mouth over his and tried to open his lips. For a moment he was tempted, but again she reminded him of Buttons. His third wife had had that same trick of biting his lower lip. It had infuriated him. Blayne moved his hands slowly up Moira's back to her hair, stroked the blonde curls with a fleeting sigh for auld lang syne, and then gave a good hard pull.

Furious, she sat up and slapped him.

"Your technique leaves something to be desired, my angel." *His* slap was not gentle. It was a well-directed stinging blow that brought tears to her eyes.

"I hate you!" she sobbed. And they were real tears.

"No, darling." Blayne rose, feeling pleased with his prudence and chastity. "You hate yourself for misjudging me."

"I thought—"

"I know what you thought, but fortunately for you, I am looking for a serene and magnificent woman who resembles the late Queen Alexandra, with the mental equipment of Madame

Curie. You do not meet either qualification. Now shall we play this straight?"

Her answer was a shrug. "O.K.," she said, "so I've always thought geniuses were dumb."

"There isn't any friend," Blayne told her politely as he crossed to the quilted-leather soundproof door. "And there isn't going to be a retainer."

Misty was waiting for him in the chartreuse hall; together playwright and poodle strolled toward the foyer, where Neddy had left his hat. Helplessly Moira followed and watched them enter the private lift. "My dear," he bowed, "consult Polti. There are only thirty-six dramatic situations, all of them an old story to me. If your problem happens to be entertaining, that will be compensation enough."

"Who is Polti?" she asked uncertainly.

"Never mind. Let me have a look at you."

For the first time she let him search her face. Were the sapphire eyes as honest as he had thought?

"Timor mortis," Blayne heard his own voice murmur. *"Timor mortis conturbat me.* If you should decide to tell me the truth, Moira, you can get in touch with me again. Otherwise, I can't help you." He started to push the button marked "Down."

But she clutched at his hand. "How does that translate, Neddy?"

As the elevator door slid slowly shut he answered. "The fear of death disturbs me. But something else disturbs you more."

When Moira Ryan was left alone in the apartment, her first gesture was to kick off her fifty-dollar Grecian sandals and take a slug of gin. Then she ran to the phone in her bedroom, an enormous room done in gold and white and honey-beige with Empire furniture, a false fireplace made of mirrors, and an oversized bed with a Napoleonic complex and gold eagles. Max's taste or a decorator's? She had never asked. The telephone was gold-plated and stood on a small table by the bed. "Gladys, have you had any messages for me?"

"Yeah. Mr. Vienna told me to tell you he took the plane to Pittsburgh. He'll be back in a couple of days." The chief operator's voice held an obscure note of triumph.

It was so typical of Max to go off without letting her know and it had happened so often that Moira was only slightly annoyed until she remembered that Dora and Albert Nates, the English servants, were gone for the night. The apartment suddenly seemed empty. Although she disliked and distrusted the Nates', they were at least human beings; they were better than nothing, better than silence and the unknown.

Barefooted on the oyster-white carpet, she went quickly from room to room turning on the lights—her habit lately when Max was gone. She locked the service door, the kitchen door, the front door, the terrace door. A sheer drop of twenty-seven stories from the terrace to the street... How many of the hotel employees had passkeys? The housekeeper? The engineer? The manager? Ridiculous to be nervous. But she wished desperately that Ida would come back and spend the night. Where was Ida?

Silly question, silly answer. Ida is a sturgeon. Remember when you worked in the same night club with Dwight Fiske? Now relax and have a drink. That's better, isn't it? Why not get into bed and turn the radio up high? Read a bit and take a sleeping pill. Don't listen for noises. Why didn't you tell Blayne? But Ida will be home pretty soon. Wait for Ida.

She held out for more than an hour. It was seven o'clock before she placed a long-distance call to Colonel James Hardquist, headmaster of the Ashford Military Academy in Ashford, Connecticut, and waited while she imagined Colonel Hardquist's annoyance at being disturbed during his roast beef, baked potatoes, green beans, and chocolate ice cream.

The crisp voice was polite but formal. "Ronnie? He's quite well, yes. Has he been writing you anything to—"

"Oh, no," she interrupted. "You know mothers."

An unamused laugh came along the other end of the wire.

"I wondered if my maid was there at the school this afternoon. I sent her with some laundry and things for Ronnie."

"Just a moment, Mrs. Ryan, I'll check." A pause. Footsteps, a door opening, vague voices. "Yes, she was here, Mrs. Ryan—very briefly. Saw Ronnie, delivered some packages to him, and left immediately."

"What time was that?"

He couldn't say exactly. "I remember Ronnie asked to be excused to go out to the driveway about teatime."

"I see. Well, thank you very much, Colonel." Moira tried to think of something suitably military and found herself saying, "Give my love to Ronnie." It was silly, of course, but after all, he was only nine. Would the Colonel summon Corporal Ryan to his office and keep the child waiting in his dress uniform with white gloves? She could see the brown eyes wondering, What kind of hot water am I in now? The salute. The stiff little back at attention.

"Corporal Ryan, I have been instructed to deliver your mother's love."

"Thank you, sir. Is that all, sir?"

Ronnie should be with her; she knew it. But Max didn't like the idea, and Max ...

What am I stalling for? Call the police, tell them. I want to report a missing car. You mean stolen? Oh, no. Now calmly. My maid should have been back here by dinnertime. Describe the car. Describe Ida. What was she wearing? I can't remember. I was too frightened. No, don't say that. Don't tell them I sent Ida in my place because when I went to the garage I thought someone was there watching me. Ida wouldn't steal my car. She's been with me too long, I trust her. Oh, she's about my size, five feet three, forty-ish, dyed blonde, not very attractive. No, I can't tell you what she had on, probably something of mine. Don't tell them that. Of course I know Ida borrows my clothes and she knows I know it, but today I can't remember. I thought there were eyes watching me so I came back to the apartment and Ida gave me brandy. I was shaking so I couldn't have driven. But I didn't want to disappoint Ronnie so Ida went and she's not back yet. I checked with the school, and she left there about tea-time. See? Nothing to it, if you keep it perfectly simple and straightforward. Don't tell them all the things that go on here, the jardiniers that move of their own accord, the bells that ring and no one's there, the moaning sounds in the middle of the night. Just report your car's missing and you think maybe Ida might have had an accident.

Then she had a better idea, which not only gave her something active to do but provided an excuse to leave the penthouse. Funny to live in the midst of eight million people and not know anyone you could visit or ask to stay with you. Not one friend. Only Ida. She decided to go to Ida's place and wait for her there. No reason to worry. Silly to worry. She probably stopped somewhere for a drink and dinner.

In her haste Moira did not notice that one of the mirrored doors in her dressing room was standing ajar—at least not at first, not until she had reached for her mink coat and could not find it. Her other furs, street clothes, sport clothes, dinner dresses, evening gowns were all there. Twice, frantically, she tore through the closet and ransacked the drawers that held her jewelry. Only the mink was missing.

Terror seized her and an icy sweat drenched her body as she became aware of the naked intensity of the emotion. This was what Blayne had meant, what he had seen in her eyes and diagnosed; this was the fear of death. She knew then, without knowing why, that she must leave the penthouse at once. Take Max's car and go. Get out of town. No note, no leave-taking.

It would be quicker to get the Derham herself, drive to some small town outside New York, and leave the conspicuous custom-built job in a parking lot. Call Max long-distance and explain. Her mind was racing with ways and means of escape as she took the private lift down to the garage.

There a vast subterranean chamber housed the black and gray and dubonnet monsters with chromium eyes that watched Moira as she ran down the center aisle searching for the Derham. Behind her, at the far end of the low-ceilinged cement cavern, almost a city block away, was the platform elevator that brought the automobiles down from the street level. No stairs, no ramp, no other exit except the passenger lift, which had already been summoned from above.

Suddenly she stopped and listened. Were they her own foot-steps that still echoed? Or another's? She walked on, beautiful nylon legs moving fast, wanting to run, high heels clicking, then stopping abruptly. The other sound stopped too, but not quite on the beat, not soon enough. Then she hadn't made it up this time, she had been right earlier in the afternoon. Now, however, it was impossible to go back to the penthouse; there was no Ida wait-ing with brandy, no safety there. They were not imaginary eyes, not chromium eyes, but real eyes watching her, eyes belonging to someone hidden behind the cars, someone who moved when she moved, toward the same objective.

She heard a groaning noise and vaguely recognized it as the big elevator beginning its slow descent. There were three levels in the garage. Moira, on the third and lowest level, shrank against an iron girder and waited. Make it come all the way down, she prayed. Make the automatic doors open and a car slide out driven by a nice kid in white overalls and I will ask him to get the Derham and take me up .... But the elevator stopped on the second level, and after a moment (long enough to die in) went up again. There was a phone on the wall somewhere but she could not remember where. Standing midway of the long corridor of cars, Moira knew paralysis, knew she could not run, for there was no place to run to. This was a trap shrewdly chosen.

Both hunter and hunted started to move at the same instant. It had finally occurred to Moira that she need not find Max's car. Any car would do to hide in. This one beside her. Sobbing and panting for breath, she squeezed past the fender. No, not a convertible—the canvas top could be slit with a knife. Not a sedan— too many doors to lock. She no longer listened for the other footsteps or heard her own, echoing wildly. A station wagon. No. She knew exactly what she wanted now and looked for it with a sort of calculating frenzy—a coupé. Run, run, run! No, not this one, the next one. Oh, God, let the windows be closed, I'll never ask anything else. But the handle wouldn't turn; it stuck. Clawing at it, she dropped her purse. She could hear him coming closer with a sort of shuffling, sliding sound. Was he behind the car? Grit on cement. He must be stepping sideways between two cars. Near, quite near. The handle wouldn't turn.

From someplace she heard a terrible noise of screaming as the door gave suddenly and she fell forward onto the seat. There were her legs to be got in somehow and the door to be closed, the left window to raise—but she had forgotten something. The two little buttons that worked the locks. So many things to do and no time to do them. And then time stopped. There was no sensation left.

How much later? She would never know. She awakened crouching under the dashboard on the floor of a strange car, panting like a sick animal, awakened to see the handle of the door turn silently. Above the handle the glass was dark. Someone was standing there, looking in, looking down at her.

In the dim light she could not make out a face, only the eyes peering down. Eyes under a hat brim. The rest of the face was covered; he was holding something to hide the lower part of his face. It was her purse. She recognized her black patent-leather purse, which she had dropped.

The handle of the door turned again, but the door did not open. So she *had* managed to lock it. Only a sheet of glass separated them, but it was enough.

The eyes under the hat brim gazed into the eyes of the stricken woman, their faces no more than a foot apart. Then, did she imagine it or was it horribly true that he closed one eye, that he winked at her in a sort of conspiratorial acknowledgment of her victory? Afterward she could not be sure that he had actually winked, but she was never to lose the feeling of that moment. From the staring eyes she had received the very definite impression of deranged glee.

Sebastian Blayne planned to stay at home that evening and wait for Mrs. Ryan's call, knowing that she would summon him again when her inner struggle became obsessive. Afraid to talk and afraid not to, she could not postpone the decision forever; some unknown factor must inevitably upset the frozen balance. What this factor would be Blayne had no way of foreseeing, and yet, dining alone in his suite, he found that he was exceedingly restless and kept glancing uneasily from the clock to the phone. He had even contrived to get rid of his two chaperons, who in their wisdom assumed they had pulled off a neat trick themselves.

"If you want to escape Neddy, there's one safe way," the secretary explained to her Italian accomplice over cocktails at Sardi's. "Threaten him with a double feature."

"Is that why he decided to work tonight?" The plump little valet chuckled. "Did he tell you anything about his cocktail assignation?"

"Absolutely mum." The redheaded secretary studied the profiles of stage luminaries on a nearby wall. "So he must have something up his sleeve."

"I know he tried to reach Lieutenant Fennelley and then changed his mind," Beppo contributed.

"Damn Fennelley. The last time Neddy not only caught cold, if you remember, but fell two chapters behind."

"There are no colds in California," Beppo said, ordering another round of Daiquiris, "according to the Chamber of Commerce. How did your day go?"

"I saw Perch." The redhead sounded pleased with herself. "Mission accomplished."

"And I saw Alvyn."

"Well?"

Beppo squinted his eyes and looked inscrutable. "It was a leetle difficult to make Syd Alvyn understand the connection. There is a blonde in a penthouse and a play that will not be finished in time for production next fall. Why? Syd wants to know. Because a book of essays for Harley Perch has been promised this spring. The books comes first. But Neddy will not work. So what do we do? Syd is asking." Beppo's imitation of the Broadway producer was devastating. "We cannot remove the blonde, I say. So we remove Neddy from the blonde. We take him to Hollywood. There he will finish the essays in time and thus be able to work on the play that Syd wants to produce in the fall."

"Did Syd buy it?"

"He promised to call Lustig long-distance and persuade him to make a picture out of one of Neddy's books. Of course, Neddy would insist on going out there to keep an eye on things."

Maggie took off her toreador's hat and flourished it. "Olé! We've done it. Jerome Lustig presents: 'Time's Fool.' I can see it."

"Not yet, Ma-gee. Neddy may not let Lustig have it. This book he loves. One day I watched him take a copy of 'Time's Fool' from the shelves. He read the first page, but only the first page, mind you, and put it back. And he said to me, 'Beppo, since I wrote that novel, more than thirty years ago, I have never opened it. It's still too close, too painful.' And there were tears in his eyes."

"He'll let them do it, never fret," Maggie was confident, "if only to show them how to make a movie. I wonder if he could persuade Bette Davis—"

"Don't be stupid. Tallulah. It's made for Tallulah."

The secretary's eyes gazed past Sardi's caricatures of theatrical comets and fallen stars far into space; in fact, as far as California. "I'll need a gabardine suit," she said.

In their clever and circuitous efforts to outwit fate, Blayne's loyal friends were inclined to forget that the Long Arm can be the best contriver of all, reaching out where and when it chooses, picking the right pawns and setting up circumstances to suit its own purposes. While Maggie and Beppo waited to hear from Hollywood, Sebastian Blayne also waited. He waited for nearly two days, but Moira Ryan did not call. Finally curiosity outweighed his vanity, prompting Neddy to make inquiries, very casual inquiries, of Beppo, who could always tap the back-stairs grapevine.

"Mrs. Ryan," the valet reported, "has been ill. Fainted in the garage, I hear. Nothing serious."

Nothing serious? Blayne wondered. "Are healthy young women of today given to the vapors of Victorian heroines? Who, may I ask, is your intelligence agent?"

"One of the elevator boys," Beppo said. "He's a friend of Nates, her butler."

"Has anyone seen Mrs. Ryan around the hotel?"

The Italian shrugged and held out his hands, palms up. That evening, Sebastian Blayne wandered aimlessly around the three luxurious rooms that he called home. He tried reading, he tried the new Poulenc album, he even tried to work, but his pen kept forming the initials M. R. Several times Neddy made up his mind to go out, but didn't.

The message he was subconsciously anticipating was late in coming, for it had to travel in a roundabout way through many strangers. First there was a young woman sitting at a bar some twenty miles away from the Park Carlton, at a roadhouse called the Blue Boar. It was about seven o'clock.

This young woman, a brunette babe in a Persian-lamb coat, was getting herself loaded and giving the bartender a bad time. Brooding over a bourbon Old-Fashioned, she was intent on one subject. "George, you oughta look into that like I told you. Where's the boss?"

"He's out. And my name isn't George, madam."

"O.K., George, but seriously, you oughta look into it."

"We have a suggestion box if you'd care to make any—"

"Now, honey, don't get elegant. I'm only telling you this for your own good. I mean the Blue Boar's good. You should excuse the expression, but there's a smell in there that'd raise the dead. You oughta report it, George, hear me? It was out of order last night when I was here. That's nearly two days. And if I gotta be brutally frank, it stinks."

"The customer is always right." The bartender sighed and removed his apron. "Hey, Harry, I'm taking five. Now, madam, which powder room was it? Upstairs or downstairs?"

At a quarter of eight one of twelve operators on the big switchboard at police headquarters took the call from the bartender at the Blue Boar Inn.

"I want to report a body."

"O.K. Anybody you know?" The young policeman winked at the officer on his right. "Anybody you know?" was a standard joke with the switchboard boys, whose job it was to screen out the crackpots and nuisances, hysterical women and high-school pranksters.

"Never saw her before. Just went in there and found her in the can. She's dead."

"Maybe she's just passed out."

"No, she's dead, all right. The toilet's been out of order for two days and all that time she's been—"

"Any identification?"

"Nah. All I know is she's wearing a feathered hat and a knife in her back."

"O.K. I'll connect you with Homicide." The operator plugged in and waited until he heard a receiver lifted and a familiar voice answer.

"Fennelley speaking."

A short time later the same man on the switchboard dialed an outside number for Lieutenant Fennelley and forgot to close his key.

"Looks like quite a case, Neddy. Want to come along?"

"To see an unidentified female cadaver wearing feathers and several inches of steel between her shoulder blades, propped up in a toilet?"

"Forget it, then. Anyway, looks like we're in for some bad weather. Paper says it might snow."

"Don't be ridiculous, Simon. Of course I'm going. Indubitably. Wouldn't miss it."

"What will Maggie say?" Fennelley asked tentatively.

"You know what you can do with Maggie," Blayne replied. "And she'd probably love it."

"All right. Pick you up on the way. Can you be waiting at the service entrance of your hotel?"

"If I can find Misty's raincoat. And Simon—do bring a squad car with a siren. I love a siren."

The Blue Boar Inn was a rambling structure, its eaves outlined in blue neon with a great electric animal resembling a buffalo on the roof. A gravel parking lot in front, a gawdy porte-cochere, a uniformed doorman. It was quite a swank establishment, Blayne decided, choosing the descriptive adjective with regurgitative care. "A place of spurious chic," he pointed out to Fennelley. "A maid's delight on her night out."

"Anyway, it's a clip joint," Fennelley said.

Simon Fennelley, an awkward six foot three, resembled Abraham Lincoln, but was better looking. A.B., Ll.B., thirty-eight. Formerly a major in the Air Force, later a special investigator in the Secret Service. Unmarried. Apartment in Greenwich

Village. Stooges, tipsters, pimps, whores, reporters, pansies, and denizens of the underworld universally respected him. They called him a square but also a square-shooter. Simon's only drawback was his basic sympathy for humanity; he was too nice to be a cop.

After the Lieutenant and Blayne had entered the fetid little room marked "Ladies," Neddy thought he was going to be sick. "There are no crimes, however great, that on certain days I have not felt capable of committing. I think that's Goethe. Heretofore I've agreed with him—but no more," he said.

There were two booths side by side in this gray-walled and sour place of death. In the far booth a woman was squatting, her feet in the toilet bowl, knees drawn up, head hanging face down between spraddled legs. "Someone," Neddy continued, "took care that her feet would not show beneath the door."

The Lieutenant nodded agreement and handed him a paste-board sign.

DANCING
At the Blue Boar Inn
Friday, Saturday, and Sunday Nights
MUSIC
by
SONNY SUNDERLAND AND HIS BLUE BOYS

On the other side was printed in large penciled block letters: OUT OF ORDER. "We found this on the toilet door," Fennelley said.

"A nice feeling for improvisation."

"What do you think of the printing?"

"Looks like mine," the writer offered. "Terrible. Any fingerprints?"

"No. None anywhere."

"Fingerprints are *démodé*, I gather?"

"Decidedly," said Simon, and offered Blayne a cigarette, which the older man accepted because of the odor in the airless room.

"Simon, would you mind closing that door? The sight of that poor woman appalls me."

The Lieutenant complied after searching the body. "No laundry marks, no cleaning tags, no labels. Her shoes and underwear from Gimbel's."

"Her dress is expensive," Blayne said when they had gone outside.

"But old. Hard to trace."

"Find her purse?"

Fennelley looked at his assistant's report. "Not yet." They passed the coroner and photographer in the hall. "You can go ahead, boys. I'll be waiting in the manager's office."

The evening dragged by while the Lieutenant questioned the staff and clients of the Blue Boar, dismissing all but the bartender. "You might get something more out of him, Neddy. Like to try?"

It was an assignment that appealed to the playwright. With the bar empty of customers and the juke box playing a clarinet arrangement of "Stardust," Blayne ordered a Courvoisier while he watched the coroner's men bear a wicker basket out into the January night. It had started to snow. The flakes fell on the long basket and melted. What pain had ended here in this neon paradise, what tragedy been played out? What kind of life had reached its end so violently, vulgarly? Blayne wondered. A knife in the back: classic symbol of betrayal. The use of the toilet: cold-blooded, no qualms. Removal of the purse and all clues of identity: sound thinking. Premeditated, then? Not necessarily. But fast work. Why the ladies' room? Was the murderer a lady? "Did you ever see the dead woman before?" he asked the bartender.

"Here?" The man known as George gestured with his thumb toward the basket going out the door. "I dunno. They don't look like live people. I mean," he fumbled, "stiffs lose all their personality. They're not the same."

"But you'd know her if she'd been a regular customer?"

"Oh, sure. At least, I think so. Maybe she was in here a few times, but I couldn't swear to it. Seems like I remember her sitting right where you are, wearing a fur coat and drinking Scotch Mists."

"What kind of fur?"

"Oh, brown."

"You're not married?"

"Huh?"

"Any married man understands the difference between mink and dyed muskrat. What is a Scotch Mist?"

"Shaved ice, Scotch, and you wave some lemon peel over it. Now you got me thinking about it, seems like she come in here a couple times with another dame. But there're so many." George wiped the sweat off his upper lip with a bar towel. "I couldn't say."

"Couldn't or wouldn't," Blayne reported later to Fennelley. "What's new with you?"

The police lieutenant dug into his sagging coat pockets and brought out a handful of scribbled notes. "The weapon—just an ordinary bread knife. Might have come out of the kitchen here—any restaurant or house, for that matter."

"What happened to her coat?"

"She wasn't wearing a coat."

"In January?"

Fennelley shrugged. "No coat and no purse—yet."

"Didn't you mention a hat?"

"Yes, but it's pretty bedraggled."

"A hat is the most revealing clue to a woman's personality," Neddy pontificated.

"Don't know what you could tell from this one." Fennelley called his assistant, Sergeant Lehny, who produced the hat—a damp sodden mass of coque feathers.

"Very smart." Blayne examined this exhibit with reverent attention. "Lilly Daché," he murmured. "Odd."

"What's odd?"

"Well, in your vernacular, Simon, they don't figure—Gimbel shoes, old dress, and this bonnet. The millinery is out of character."

"Where does that get us?"

"It's an original. Lilly might remember who bought it. I'll call her tomorrow."

But as it turned out, there was no necessity for Miss Daché to identify the corpse's hat. Someone else was able to identify the corpse—with the help of Mistinguett. Not that Misty meant to help. On the contrary, the distinguished poodle was in a very un-co-operative mood when Blayne found her hiding under the desk in the manager's office. "Why so haughty, old girl?"

Misty had no reply to make. Scratching behind the ears, fondling the topknot, murmuring baby dog talk—all was to no avail. Misty implied with a look that she had been ignored, cast aside like a mongrel, and generally humiliated. A few sirloin scraps from the kitchen were not welcome, but they did not make up for the ignominy of being imprisoned in the ladies' room, where she had followed Neddy, and where she had been trapped.

"It's no use," he sighed. "She won't speak to me for days. I once had a wife who punished me like that." Then he noticed a small object between Misty's front paws. In spite of the dog's caterwauling, the bit of cardboard was still legible. It was a Gimbel charge-account card. Number 6029543. "Where did you pick this up, angel-puss?" Blayne inquired, but Mistinguett kept her own council.

"I'll check that number," Fennelley said, and gave the poodle an appreciative but casual pat, for which she nuzzled him extravagantly. Misty's moment of glory was brief though. The phone rang and claimed the Lieutenant's attention with a report from the coroner. In the small office a metallic voice issued clearly from the receiver.

"Si? Got news for you."

"Already?"

"Haven't finished the autopsy yet, but thought you'd like to know. This is a weirdy. Two wounds, see? A deep one, which was fatal—and a very shallow one. They're about a sixteenth of an inch apart."

"So he struck twice? Why not?"

"But I got the knife out of the second one. It's not much of an incision. The first jab went straight to the heart."

Blayne interrupted. "He might have removed the weapon, changed his mind, and decided to replace it."

"Or substituted the kitchen knife for the real one that killed her," Fennelley suggested.

The metallic voice said, "Could be. That's your department."

"How long has she been dead?"

"Oh, the usual, Si. Indeterminate. Maybe thirty-six to forty-eight hours. Maybe longer."

"Can't you be more definite?"

"Not in this weather, sweetheart. Have you looked at the thermometer?"

After Fennelley had hung up, Blayne discovered the coroner was right about the falling temperature. Sergeant Lehny beckoned the Lieutenant outside to the parking lot, and Neddy, forgetting his overcoat, tagged along. At the back of the lot in lonely splendor stood a baby-blue Cadillac dusted with snow.

"This is it, sir." Fondly Fennelley's assistant patted its left fish tail. "Have you any idea, Mr. Blayne, how many cars are stolen every day in the five boroughs of New York City?"

"Now really," the armchair criminologist protested, longing for his armchair. "If you've lured me out here to play Twenty Questions—"

"Yesterday," the Sergeant announced, referring to a moist note pad, "there were seven hundred and twenty-one vehicles."

"I am impressed," Blayne sneezed, "but the evening is wearing on and it is now five degrees above zero. As far as I am concerned, statistics can wait."

"This particular car," Fennelley said, "was reported missing only a few hours ago."

"Splendid. My congratulations to the entire force. And now if I may suggest a drink of—"

"The person who reported the theft refused to give a name. There may be some connection."

"With your closet corpse?" Blayne sneezed again and retreated toward the night-club entrance.

"Probably not. But we'll check. Who is the owner, Lehny?"

"The registered owner," the Sergeant consulted his notebook, "is a party called Mrs. Moira Ryan."

Neddy's well-known eyebrow shot up, cocking itself in an involuntary exclamation point, but Fennelley unfortunately missed it. On three continents Sebastian Blayne's eyebrow was recognized as a dead giveaway to the inner man.

The inner man had just yelled, "Wow!" but Neddy quickly covered for him. "As Bob Benchley, God bless him, once said, let's get out of these wet clothes and into a dry Martini."

CHAPTER THREE

After leaving the Blue Boar Inn, Sebastian Blayne could never quite remember the events of that stormy night in their exact time sequence. During the drive back to town he had begun to sneeze and cough and they had stopped somewhere (hadn't they?) for antihistamine tablets. Drowsy from pills and potions, lulled by the vibration of the car and the hypnotic quality of the falling snow, he had let himself steal away from the tired old Blayne body, drifting into a kind of false state of suspended consciousness that was neither waking nor sleeping, in which it seemed to Neddy that Simon was terribly busy talking on the car telephone to numerous people and that the ride home was taking longer than it should.

Had they gone to the morgue, or did he dream of that white-tiled corridor leading to an icy room filled with the stench of formaldehyde and the glare of a bright electric bulb revealing the pitiful mottled flesh of a middle-aged female? And then Fennelley's voice saying, "I checked with Gimbel's. They're open late tonight. That charge account belonged to Ida Gibbons."

Ah, that was it, Neddy thought, that painting. "There Came into the World a Soul Called Ida." Obese thighs, moribund and evil. Purplish-green shadows. A soul called Ida. Unforgettable refrain. A soul called Ida. Or was it only a nightmare? No, he had stared at the woman's face this time, the woman who had traveled in a wicker basket from the Blue Boar to this narrow zinc-lined locker drawer. Surely he had heard Fennelley say, "her name was Ida Gibbons. In Gimbel's files the credit reference was…" Yes, he had studied her face and remembered thinking she was surprised; not hurt or horrified, but horribly surprised. "The credit reference was Mrs. Moira Ryan."

Then Misty had wanted to go home to bed but they had driven somewhere else, a long cold way across town to the dead woman's apartment, and Fennelley had examined the clothes in her closet and found her purse. Dreary little place with food and dirty dishes standing about and the bed unmade. The sergeant called Lehny had given him another of those capsules and a glass of water with bourbon. And all the while he had been wondering if he should tell his friend Simon about Moira or warn Moira before she met Fennelley.

With every passing minute an explanation seemed increasingly difficult. Why had he waited to speak? The sin of omission, Neddy thought, and now the unsaid became a lie. In the parking lot when they first found the baby-blue Cadillac, that had been the time. Now the right time had passed and he allowed himself to become even more deeply involved.

On the way home to the Park Carlton the Lieutenant said, "She lives at your hotel, oddly enough. Think I'll run up and see her."

He remembered the rest of it quite clearly, remembered saying with a yawn, "She's probably asleep. Won't tomorrow morning be soon enough?"

"I want her to identify the body."

"Really, Simon, that's a gruesome shock to anyone, particularly a woman—to be awakened in the middle of the night by the police and summoned to the morgue in a snowstorm."

They had left it at that, and the next thing Neddy knew he and his dog were walking through the hothouse-flower-scented empty lobby, bowing to the night clerk, and riding up in the elevator past his own floor, and then his gray suede glove was pressing the doorbell to the penthouse, and Moira's wide alarmed eyes were facing him.

When they were sitting in the make-believe night club with
its amber spotlight Blayne adroitly led up to the question of Ida
Gibbons.

"I heard it on the radio," she said harshly. "Ida was the nearest thing to a friend—" Her voice broke and she took a long time
opening a bottle of Scotch. "Poor old thing, she shouldn't have
borrowed my hat."

On his astral plane this made no sense to Neddy.

"I've made up my mind to tell you the truth," she went on.

And Neddy heard vaguely something about the hotel garage
and a man's eyes gleaming insanely through the car window.

"But this isn't the first time," she added. "There have been
other attempts. Someone keeps trying."

"To get rid of you, eh?" Blayne smiled wisely.

"Or make me leave Max. Why should I? Max is worth nine
million."

"Then you certainly have nine million good reasons to stick
around. Now, uh—" He sat up very straight and tried to think
without letting the effort show. "Who is this someone? Any idea?"

"It might be Josie. Max has never got a divorce from his wife.
She's a frightening kind of person. But then naturally I hate her."

Ah, thought Blayne, at last.

The smoke from her cigarette rose in a straight blue column
and Moira stared at it as she spoke. "There're so many people," she
went on quietly, "who want to prevent our marriage. His mother,
for instance. She's an awful old thing. All wrinkles with hands
like claws—simply horrid. And there's a two-headed brother
called Felix. Actually I suppose he's a sort of gangster."

"Is he horrid too?"

"I know what you're thinking. They can't all be horrid. But
they are."

Blayne's attention began to wander. The room was warm and
the amber light soothing; the night's activities had exhausted
him. He was unbearably sleepy. Where was Misty? It was high

time they went home. From far away he heard Moira going on and on about Max and Max's family; the wife, the wife's lover... Anyway, someone had a lover by the revolting name of Igor. Too much plot, Neddy decided. Only wisps of words and phrases reached him. What was he doing here when he couldn't care less?

"Are you falling asleep in my face?" she accused.

"Don't be ridiculous. Always close my eyes when I'm concentrating. Go on."

She did not have to be urged. "Before Max—" She looked beyond Blayne's shoulder into another place and time. "I worked in several clubs and a couple of musical comedies—bits. Never set the world on fire, but it was a living. Better than a row house in Philadelphia. You see why Jay impressed me. The right school, the right clothes, the right kind of family. Jason Ryan, Yale and Long Island. I was nineteen and he was twenty-three. His father made a down payment on a house for us. You know the kind— a colonial entrance and cheap plumbing. White ruffly curtains and no shrubbery. God. Babes in Toyland. Five months later a van drove up and removed the furniture."

"The honeymoon was obviously over," Blayne commented, wondering where he had left his hat and Misty.

"We lost not only the imitation Duncan Phyfe and the house, but our friends. They seemed to melt away. Then his father died and the wake lasted over a year. Jay went from Scotch to rye to gin. From five-hundred-dollar loans to twenty-dollar touches to cadging a buck. Jay was the sweetest, the most thoughtful, the most adorable bastard you can possibly imagine. Strange how you can't remember love when it stops." She reached for another drink and filled Blayne's glass. "I was pregnant, and he continued to buy his clothes from Brooks Brothers. Pawned everything we owned—my wedding presents, even my grandmother's little pearl brooch. I don't know why I should justify myself to you, but somehow I wanted you to understand why—how I was trapped."

Blayne brought his head back to a perpendicular position and blinked. "I do not have a censorious nature, Moira darling. Living is too difficult. We all live as we can. Go back to the time you first met Max Vienna and liked his money."

"I liked *him*."

"Very well, you liked him—but one must be provident."

"Max sent me to Reno and paid for my divorce and the baby." Her face brightened. "Oh, I want you to meet Ronnie, he's an angel."

"Where do you keep this angel?"

"*How* I've managed to keep him is the real point. You don't know what it is to grub for pennies. I tried being a waitress."

"I was not born with a platinum porringer, my girl. At sixteen I was a clerk in a shipping office, three and ten a week."

"Could you go back to that?"

As an alternative Neddy tried to think of himself as a kept woman. The whole idea became so amusing that he forgot Moira and chuckled.

"Are you laughing at me?"

Blayne sighed, swallowed his Scotch neat with another cold capsule, thought of tomorrow's hangover, and gave up any hope of bed. "Give me the full treatment," he said. "And don't skip."

For fully three minutes Neddy followed Moira before the agonizing slumber began again.

"A man in the park ... years ago ... stepped out of the bushes and made a grab at the reins. The horse reared and I was thrown. Spinal injury ... detective ... thought I made it up ...."

With enormous effort Blayne jerked his mind back from the sweet depths. "A sex maniac, maybe?"

She shrugged. "That's what *they* said. The police. The whole matter was filed and forgotten."

The depths claimed him again.

"Then the ball park ... A big-league game ... in the midst of a dreadful brawl about the Dodgers ... Swear I was deliberately pushed into that mob … easily trampled to death. Only my jaw broken … But Max always accuses me of imagining things."

Then he lost the narration until the word "truck." "Will you repeat that statement, please?"

"I said I couldn't have imagined the truck. It was on a bad curve—a bad night. You've seen them do it in the movies." Her hands were trembling as she diagramed the scene on the tabletop.

"What kind of truck?" Neddy knew he had to say something. "Wasn't there a name on the side or—"

Moira laughed and lighted another cigarette, chain-smoking. "Of course. While I crashed through the retaining wall and landed upside down in the ravine, I was able to jot down the driver's license number, age, weight, and the color of his eyes."

Her sarcasm turned the trick. "Too bad you couldn't have made a notation of his nationality and religious affiliations." Neddy was awake enough now to reach for the Heather Dew. "Your accidents seem to have considerable variety, and I might even say artistry. Did you report this one?"

She hedged. "No, because I wasn't badly hurt. A miracle, really. My car was absolutely ruined, but I—"

"You didn't report it because the police will not ignore a hit-and-run accident. Are you afraid of reprisals?"

She did not meet his eyes. Then he noticed that she was staring over his shoulder again. The smoke from her cigarette was no longer a straight single column but broken curlicues. There must be a draft. Neddy made this remarkable deduction before he remembered there were no windows in Max Vienna's imitation night club. His companion's hand reached for his and nails bit into his flesh. Her lips barely moved and she spoke in a voice so faint that it was hardly a voice at all. "Don't look around. Go on talking about something else."

He responded automatically. "I have always been good at dialogue, you know," Blayne replied in his normal clipped tone. "What subject would you prefer?"

"The door is opening," she whispered. "Someone is listening." And then she said aloud with a social lilt, "What I'd really like to hear about is your new play."

He allowed his eyes to turn briefly, obliquely toward the hall door. It was opening very slowly and cautiously, a white leather door with black mirrors for buttons.

"I don't know that I shall live to write another play," Neddy said, for want of something better. There was perspiration on his forehead. The unbearable silence lengthened, a silence that even Blayne could not fill. If ever I had words, let me use them now, he prayed, but none came. The tremor in Moira Ryan's hands increased as she lifted her drink.

A head appeared around the door. The glass dropped from her hand and shattered.

The head belonged to a gray French poodle, looking very injured, very neglected. Mistinguett thrust the door farther open and announced her displeasure with a short, aggrieved, utterly feminine little bark.

"You bitch," said Blayne, but he could have kissed her.

It was too late, Sebastian Blayne decided, to face an elevator boy. He would walk downstairs to his own floor. Mustn't compromise a lady. What had he promised to do tomorrow? Take care of her, that was it. More than a little delirious with a high fever, sore throat, Heather Dew, and antihistamine, Neddy recognized that the descent to his eighth-floor apartment was taking on a surrealist quality. Somehow a great many floors floated and slid by him before he and Misty found themselves on the street level. Obviously it would be silly if not impossible to go up again. A better idea was born.

CHAPTER FOUR

Alone in the penthouse, Moira Ryan was reassured by the fact that Blayne was at least with her in spirit. She knew he was interested in what he called the "situation at rise," or he would not have called on her at such an hour. As she undressed she felt almost safe, almost as if nothing else could happen now. Blayne lived in the same building; she had only to pick up the phone if... Of course, his manner had been somewhat odd, but then writers *were* odd, and he had promised to help her.

In the mirrored dressing room Max Vienna's mistress surveyed her naked white image thrice reflected, front, back, and profile. The weapons of a woman are too vulnerable, she thought. There's only one way we can fight back. She reached for her robe. Then all her new-found confidence left her, all the Scotch and false courage drained out of her blood in one heart-stopping second.

On its usual padded satin hanger hung her mink coat. The coat that had been stolen. I couldn't have made a mistake, she thought. It wasn't there, I'm sure it wasn't there the other night. And now whoever took it has returned it. Why?

"Nice," a man's voice said behind her. "A very nice picture."

Moira whirled around, clutching her robe, to face Max Vienna. "Darling!" she cried in relief. "It's you."

He was standing in the doorway smiling. "You were expecting maybe someone else?" He crossed the thick carpet and took her in his arms.

"That's got to be a joke, son," she whispered with her face against his. "I'm so glad you're back."

"I heard a bulletin on the radio about your car. Recognized the license number. So I grabbed the first plane."

While they got ready for bed and had a nightcap she told him about Ida, without mentioning Sebastian Blayne. Or the man in the garage; for that would come under the head of "imagining things."

"So it was Ida," Max said. "The announcer said an unidentified woman—"

"I went over to her place this afternoon. I was worried about her. Funny, Ida was so neat—she left things in an awful mess."

"You should tell the police that."

"Oh, Max, please, don't make me—"

"But baby, you're not involved in this." He took their glasses across the hall to the bar and returned with fresh Scotch and sodas, dark amber for Moira, straw-colored for himself. Sitting down beside her on the bed, he asked abruptly, "You had a key to Ida's apartment? You find it a discreet place for a rendezvous?"

"Darling, you know better than that. Don't let's quarrel. I can't stand any more."

"You had someone up here tonight. The bar's a mess. Even a broken glass."

Max Vienna was a very jealous man in spite of his millions and his extraordinary appeal for women. Not tall, not short, he had the sort of lean, well-knit body that clothes hang on correctly. He was forty-five but passed easily for thirty; his smooth, closed, enigmatic face and olive skin were ageless, his features regular, his bearing distinguished. A receding hairline. Dark wavy hair. Dark curly lashes. He might have been an East Side Jew or an Oriental prince or a movie actor. The facts, which very few people knew, were more interesting. The boy-genius hotel-man had been born of a peasant family living on the outskirts of Vienna. Apprenticed to a butcher, a cobbler, a carpenter, a furrier, and finally to a restaurateur, Max had run away to America as a thirteen-year-old immigrant. It was amazing (and another proof of his talent) that he had no revealing environmental scars, no identifiable accent—only a slight Continental slur that charmingly concealed a multitude of grammatical sins.

"Who was here, Moira?" he repeated, as always pronouncing her name Mara, rolling the "r."

She did not hesitate. "It was Jay. He wanted permission to see Ronnie."

"That drunk. When did he turn up?"

"He's back here, in New York."

"Where?"

"He didn't say." She lay back against the pillows. "Now tell me about Pittsburgh."

"Never mind Pittsburgh." Max also lay back, but not on the pillows. He put his head in her lap and looked up at her face. "Don't lie. Where is he staying?"

"Darling, don't be silly." She stroked his head and they were silent for a time. "Max, the next time you go away for a few days, could I take a little trip too?"

"How little? A week end in Atlantic City with your former husband?"

"I just want to—to get out of town for a while. Get myself lost." She tried to make it sound like a feminine whim while he kissed the inside of her leg, her thighs.

Why couldn't I tell him there is a man, a man I saw in the garage who wants me dead? If I can go away and disappear maybe he won't find out he made a mistake. She was wearing my hat, I gave it to her. Blayne said he saw her in the morgue and she looked so cold. You see, they meant for me to be lying in the morgue. They meant me.

"You're upset about this Ida business. Jitters, that's all. We'll call the police tomorrow and offer to co-operate. You've got no reason to run away."

"I know, but you will let me, won't you, darling?"

For a long moment he didn't answer. She couldn't tell what he was thinking behind his strange dark eyes. "What brand of cigarette does Mr. Ryan smoke?"

"Why? How on earth would I know?"

"You must have spent quite some time with him."

"I can't remember."

"He does smoke, doesn't he?"

"Yes, but—"

"A regular brand?"

"I didn't pay any attention."

"You would have noticed an expensive off brand, wouldn't you? When he's supposed to be so broke?"

"Did I say he was broke?"

"Isn't it always a touch?"

"I suppose so."

"How much did you give him?"

"Fifty."

"Where did you get it? Never mind. Now tell me what he smokes. Melachrinos? Parliaments? Fatimas? Players? English Ovals?"

"What does it matter? Jay always used to smoke Tareytons."

"Tareytons, eh?"

"Yes, I remember—he offered me one."

"Fine. I'll send him a carton."

"Where?"

"Who cares—since we've both been lying? Jay Ryan wasn't here tonight. Now tell me who was." Then he bit the soft inner side of her leg until she screamed, and told him about Sebastian Blayne.

They quarreled bitterly and Max walked out.

The apartment on Riverside Drive that Max Vienna maintained for his mother was furnished with Persian carpets, overstuffed velour chairs, brocade draperies, and tinted pictures of Jesus, Mary, and Joseph—and Max. His gifts included a Chinese Chippendale radio-television set, a cigarette box shaped like a grand piano that played *"La Paloma"* when the lid was lifted, a refrigerator with a deep-freeze unit, a dishwasher, and an electric stove complete with clock, timer, and radio. Mamma liked the gleaming white kitchen best, and spent most of her time there in a straight rocker watching the truck deliveries in the alley.

Every morning she attended mass and in the afternoon the neighborhood movies. Except for her younger son, Felix, who checked in and out of the apartment as if it were a hotel, Mamma was alone for days at a time and was much given to reverie, that inward staring of the aged, seeking to peer through self and time for an explanation.

Max was still angry when he arrived at his mother's and awakened her. "Cheese blintzes," Mamma Vienna said, taking one look at him. "I know what you want."

"No, Mamma."

She led him into the kitchen. *"Ja, ja.* I know better." They were speaking German. No one knew quite how old Max's mother was; her history had been lost in History. The Franco-Prussian war, the First World War, and the Nazis had come and gone; ten of her children had died, but she had survived. She was under five feet tall and deceptively fragile, and her shriveled hawk's face was a net of wrinkles out of which darted beady bird's eyes. She spoke only a little English and could not read. Her costume never varied—a black silk dress, starched white apron, and lace cap to cover her sparse white hairs. So quaint, such a dear little old lady, people said.

"You look tired, *Liebling.* You ain't sick?"

"I'm all right." Max sat down on a high stool beside the refrigerator and watched the snow falling in the alley while his mother made coffee.

"So long, Maxie, we ain't seen you." Getting the cheese from the refrigerator, she paused to pat his face and kiss him. "My good boy."

"Not so good, Mamma. I'm no good to live with."

She understood that he meant Moira, whom she hated with all her medieval peasant's mind. "Better you go back to Josie." Mamma approved of Max's wife, who still paid her mother-in-law homage by regular weekly visits, automobile rides, and presents. Josephine Vienna had been a barber's assistant when Max met her during a business trip to Paris. While she lathered his chin he had admired the Frenchwoman's snapping brown eyes, succulent lips, and overripe breasts—and married her because he was lonely. Six months later they agreed to live apart.

Ten years later Josie owned three beauty shops in New York City and her own line of cosmetics, and Max still contributed a thousand a week to her support. Intended by nature to be a prostitute, she was not lazy enough, for more than her extraordinary appetites she loved money. It suited her book perfectly to be separated from Max, but a divorce did not enter her thinking. She had joined the Roman Church at the time of their marriage and did not underestimate its power. The Church, she knew, was Mamma Vienna's God. Mamma believed what the priest said about divorce, and Max believed what Mamma told him. So Josie had no idea of relinquishing a wife's interest in her husband's vast estate, or the Russian nobleman of dubious title who was her lover. Igor resembled the Romanoffs and was her partner in the beauty business. "Of course, she has other side lines," Moira once pointed out. "She has her friends and Igor has them too." But the Eager Beaver and Josie had more in common than a weakness for male hairdressers. Truly they were two minds with but a single thought, two hearts that beat as one when it came to the question of Max's money—and how they would spend it if he should die.

"Mamma," Max said, pushing the blintzes away from him, "I'm going to divorce Josie—for adultery." He used a word she would understand.

"My Maxling, he don't feel good." Mamma never heard what she did not wish to hear. "Always he worries, he don't eat, don't sleep."

He tried to tell her how much he wanted Moira, but his mother knew it wasn't her son talking, it was "that woman." "Come now, like old times I tuck you in."

"Yes, Mamma." He followed her obediently after he had emptied the plate of blintzes into the incinerator.

"Undress, Maxie, I seen you naked before."

But he wanted to smoke a cigarette and told her good night at the door.

"Give a kiss, *Liebling*." She held him with her old arms. "My son, sleep now. And when comes tomorrow we talk all about it. Sleep good."

Max Vienna stood for a long time looking out the window. The snow seemed to float. He was so tired.... Was he falling asleep or falling with the snow, endlessly falling? There were lights from a million windows and behind every light a life. Somewhere among those lights was Moira. Was she sleeping or watching the storm too?

The great flakes fell on the Park Carlton penthouse, on the sloping slate roof, the tiles of the outer terrace, the wrought-iron chairs and tables. Small fluffy blankets covered the flowerpots and there was no footstep anywhere. Clean, peaceful, undisturbed...Down below, far down below, a miniature taxi made tracks in the snow. Moira Ryan watched a Lilliputian man get out of a cab and cross the street toward the hotel.... Mamma Vienna lay awake on Riverside Drive and listened for Max's footsteps. She heard him get up and walk to the door, then go back to bed. She waited and dozed. To the door, the window, the door, the bed, the door.... Ida Gibbons slept soundly in her metal locker.

And still the snow drifted down. Softly, softly, timeless, a shroud for the towered city, and Josie Vienna suffered from insomnia because of a telephone call from Max's mother. Igor was awake when Josie called him. He arose and left his friend and went out into the night. Jay Ryan also walked the streets. He was broke and had no place to sleep. Simon Fennelley, under his overcoat and an army blanket, was trying to catch a nap on the desk in his office. It was five in the morning. Ten below zero. Great drifts blocked the streets. God help the poor taxi driver, Simon thought, and shifted uneasily. A minute later he was dreaming. But the murderer was not asleep. He was on his way—to kill again.

Moira Ryan wondered why the seconal wouldn't work. After Max left she had locked her bedroom door, but she could not talk herself out of a frantic feeling of being alone. How many hours had gone by? The clock was surely wrong. Outside her windows, which opened on nothing but black night, the skyline looked like a row of tombstones, Moira thought. She shuddered. When would it be daybreak? She could see it like a movie title: "Then the Dawn Came." She laughed out loud.

You sent Ida to her death, she accused herself. You sent her in your place, in your car, your hat. You know they want you dead. They? Who are they? If not they, who? Him. The one with the eyes looking through the car window.

The one who is coming.

Is the balustrade wide enough to hold a man if—? Could he slide down a rope from the roof? Admit it's possible. For an acrobat. You are being very, very stupid. Tomorrow I will tell Albert and Dora they must sleep in. Tomorrow when the dawn comes. I will never stay here alone again. Who was laughing?

Max, where did you go? Another woman? No, he's run home to Mamma because I hurt his precious little feelings. I lied to him about Blayne. Why can't I be honest with anyone? I didn't tell the whole truth even to Neddy.

Did you try the glass doors to the terrace, the kitchen door, the service door, the fire-escape door? Yes, but waiting is worse than going from room to room.

Don't look at the dark; the apartment is just the same. But it doesn't feel the same. Max's library. Empty. The bar. Empty. You see? You have searched every room and there is no one, silly. There never is anyone, remember? Why do you think someone has come in?

"Operator, give me Mr. Blayne's apartment."

"We have instructions not to—"

"Sebastian Blayne, please!" The ringing went on for a long time.

Oh, Neddy, answer it. God, make him pick it up and speak to me. I'm in terrible danger.

"Operator, keep trying Mr. Blayne's apartment."

"I'm sorry, there's no answer."

Am I asleep and dreaming this? I know I locked the door but there is someone in this room, tiptoeing toward me. There is someone beside the bed.

CHAPTER FIVE

Simon Fennelley stood for a long time staring at the footprints in the snow. They began at the French door and ran straight across the terrace to the balustrade, then returned. The snow on the balustrade was slightly disturbed. "Tell Sergeant Lehny I want molds of these prints," the Lieutenant grumbled in his official voice, "before anything happens to them." The harness bull said, "Yes, sir," and got out fast when he saw the boss pop a white tablet into his mouth.

It was all very well for the detective to tell himself that his pain was psychosomatic, but that did not stop the gnawing duodenal ache that became acute whenever a case worried him. And he was worried now. One woman in the morgue and another in the hospital bleeding to death internally. The Lieutenant wished the small arrogant figure of the renowned dramatist would appear in the doorway with Mistinguett and a flow of Blaynean abuse, but Neddy was not at home—or anyway, not answering the phone.

First on Fennelley's list of hotel employees to be interviewed was Gladys Scherman, the telephone operator who had called the police. She was a modern Bronx version of the old-fashioned spinster with the latest hair style and a basic black dress with pearls. Not a bad-looking thirtyish brunette, thin-hipped and acid-tongued. "How long have you been at the Park Carlton?"

"Eleven years. The last three I've been the chief operator."

"You must have heard a lot of things in your time." Simon winked at Gladys with all the finesse of an iron butterfly.

"If you're implicating that I leave my key open—"

"That's part of a chief operator's job."

"Well, Mr. Fennelley—I mean Lieutenant—" She was mollified.

"My name's Simon."

"I should know what your name is. I've been talking to you on the phone for a couple of years, taking your messages every time you call Mr. Blayne."

"Then we're really old friends."

"In a manner of speaking," she punned, and giggled.

Fennelley offered Gladys a cigarette and was charming for five minutes before he asked, "When you called headquarters, I believe you said it was a woman's voice. Could you recognize it?"

"Hardly. I was too excited. She kept whispering. 'Help, help,' like that." Gladys took a drag from her cigarette with the air of a tragic cinema queen. "Have you questioned Mrs. Vienna yet?"

Simon thought he detected a slight undercurrent of animosity. "The wife?"

"Yes. I happen to know she's got a key to the penthouse. A master key. However—" She paused, wrinkling her brows to simulate thought. "Any of the employees with a passkey could've got in. Miss Anna, the housekeeper—Mr. Prince, he's the manager—Joseph, the engineer—or even room service. And that snotty English couple."

But Fennelley was not to be side-tracked. "Tell me about the wife."

"We-l-l, Mrs. Vienna has propositioned me three or four times. I mean," Gladys hurried on, "she wanted me to listen in on the penthouse line—for quite a nice hunk of dough."

"But you wouldn't do that?"

Gladys was indignant. "I simply considered the source. My loyalty belongs to Mr. Vienna. He's my employer, and he's a *naw*-fully nice guy."

"He seems to be."

"Oh, everybody around the hotel simply adores him. Honestly, he's tops. And besides," she stretched her neck forward and mouthed the words, "he pays me to do the same job."

"Vienna pays you?"

"To check up on Ryan. Nuts about her. And I do mean nuts."

"You don't happen to know where Mr. Vienna was on the day that Ida Gibbons was killed?"

"Sure. He was in Pittsburgh. I remember because he'd been trying to get Ryan long-distance."

"Where was Mrs. Ryan?"

"I wouldn't know."

"Any other calls last night?"

"Out of the ordinary?" Gladys frowned. "We-l-l, she tried to ring one of the hotel guests—Mr. Blayne, as I remember."

"Oh?" said Fennelley with the utmost calm. "They were acquainted?"

"Just here lately. Anyway, when his room don't answer she sounds kinda funny and hangs up. Then maybe five minutes later *he* calls *her* from outside the hotel."

"Mr. Vienna?"

"No, Mr. Blayne. Or anyway, a party who says, 'I'm speaking for Mr. Blayne. Will you ring the penthouse?'"

"Could you recognize this party?"

"No, but it was a lady."

"This is getting very interesting." Fennelley might have been posing for his portrait. He was sitting ominously still.

"So I give the penthouse a buzz, but this time *she* don't answer. I mean La Ryan—you should pardon my French. After all, it's practically five in the morning. 'Would Mr. Blayne like to leave a message?' I ask the lady, and she says, 'No, thanks'; and hangs up. Then whatdaya know, Ryan's light comes on a couple seconds later, meaning someone has taken the receiver off the hook. But nobody's there. I figure she's tight or taken a pill. It's happened before. She knocks the phone off the table and don't know it."

"Then what?" Fennelley's ulcer was urging him to have words with Neddy.

"Then nothing for a while. My board gets busy and I forget about Ryan's light. Imagine! I had a front-row ticket and could've caught the whole thing, maybe. But no, I'm engaged elsewhere," Gladys finished with ironic elegance.

"How long before you heard the cry for help?"

Gladys looked vague. "Maybe ten-twenty minutes."

"You're sure you couldn't recognize the voice?"

"I couldn't swear to it."

"Never mind that. Telephone conversations never stand up in court. Who do you *think* it was?"

But Gladys refused to give. Somewhere along the line Simon knew she was lying, but where? Why had she suddenly dried up? Had the murderer taken Mrs. Ryan's phone off the hook? If so, why? He had only Gladys Scherman's word for this. There were no prints on the receiver. Wiped clean. A woman's voice had called for help. It had also been a woman's voice using Sebastian Blayne's name. If Neddy was Moira's friend, why hadn't he said so the night before?

Dismissing the telephone operator, the Lieutenant sent for Max Vienna's English butler and housekeeper, who bore the brunt of Fennelley's annoyance with Gladys and his ulcer's concern over Blayne.

After the interview with the Lieutenant both Mr. and Mrs. Nates felt the need of a consoling tumbler of Holland gin. In the pantry with the door locked, Dora inquired of her husband cautiously, "Did you make them footprints, Bertie?"

"No. Did you?" Both Bertie and his dear spouse had been born some distance from Bow bells, but their accent was none the less genuine. "We was both telling the truth?" This was a shock to Bertie Nates. "Who d'you think done it? Now, if we stay it's trouble, and if we leave it's more trouble. Between the devil and the deep."

"You're a great thinker, you are." Flurried by their unexpected summons from the police, Mrs. Nates had forgotten to put on her hearing aid, and yet, as Fennelley had noticed, she seemed to hear perfectly without it. "If you ask me, we'd better blow."

"Now, steady on, Dora, we've a good thing here."

"You mean it *has* been a good thing up to now. I don't fancy it no more, now its murder. I say we undo that jigger in the ventilating system and take down all your fancy little tricks. Tonight." Dora suddenly began to snicker. "Every time I think of Mrs. Ryan's face when one of them sounds came ooh-oohing out of the blue, I have to double up. 'Do you hear anything, Dora?' And I'd go into my dummy act—put my head on one side and listen. And I'd say, 'No, mum. I don't hear nothing.' And I'd stare right at her like she was crazy."

Mr. Nates was not amused. "I guess it was all in the way of business, but sometimes I did feel sorry for her, rather. What's to stop us from putting the bite on the wife?"

"Her? Oh, come off it, Bertie." Mrs. Nates' voice was a low snarl. "She knows we can't afford to talk."

"We could try it, anyway. She hired us."

"You always was stupid, Bertie. We've made a nice profit here. Don't be greedy. Besides, I've got the coat."

"What coat?"

"Her mink. Been wanting one all my life. Worth a pretty penny, too. We'll pack up tonight and clear out before Mr. Nosy Fennelley comes poking around again."

But Bertie Nates was stunned. "Whose coat?"

"Ryan's. I left it at Papa Kransky's on a five-dollar ticket. It'll be waiting for us just like money in the bank whenever we care to tap it. How's that?"

Bertie gave her an approving slap on the buttocks. "You may be a little rump-sprung, old girl, but I must say you're on the beam. Here, have another, dearie, and then we'll pack."

CHAPTER SIX

It seemed to Moira, tossing in delirium, that her hospital bed had been transmuted into a long mahogany table that was floating in a dim sea of pearly gray mist. Or was it water? There were several people about the table, seated on stacks of stocks. Or bonds? The stocks kept slipping in the water, sliding down and up again. Nothing would stay still. It was a stockholders' meeting, she knew that much, but why was she there?

"I am not a director of this company," Moira told them, trying to rise from the center of the table where they were holding her. "I don't belong here." And then she saw other faces that did not belong there either. Jay Ryan with his bloodshot eyes but still handsome in a white dinner coat and Tahitian bathing trunks. Nice legs, Moira decided, very nice legs.

Jay leaned forward, his face close to hers. "I still love you, darling," he murmured, "but I need money. I can't earn a living. I've tried. You'll have to keep on supporting me—or else."

"Or else what?"

"I'll give you a bad time."

"This meeting will come to order," Josie Vienna announced from her place at the head of the table, rapping with a diamond revolver. Her hair was lacquered in an up-do and she wore a seaweed stole with ermine tails. Otherwise she was naked and her breasts kept floating away and returning, swimming like round fish with nipple eyes. "We are the suspects," Josie said with her French accent, which she intensified for the occasion. "Naturally, Moira, I could kill you for taking my husband."

"You don't love Max." Moira peered at Josie's face, which kept changing shape. If only they would all be quiet for a moment, but the whole room rocked with a wavy motion and the pain came in waves too. "You were separated when I met him."

"He is my property," the wife said. "There will be no divorce."

"I agree," Jay Ryan stated.

"Then she must go." Josie shrugged. "It would be so much simpler, darling, if you were dead."

"Moira Ryan is *not* going to die." Sebastian Blayne swam into the argument, well groomed in a fashionable manuscript padded at the shoulders and sporting a red carnation.

"Oh, Neddy, where were you last night? Help me."

"It is the old problem of the locked room," Blayne answered impressively.

Moira introduced Blayne to the board of directors before she took him aside to whisper, "Neddy, the murderer had to have a key."

⚜ ⚜ ⚜

The woman in starched white left her patient to summon Max Vienna. "She keeps asking for someone by the name of Blayne."

Max said, "I'll try to get him," and sat down by Moira's bedside.

The nurse was little and blonde and a recent graduate. "She's really doing as well as can be expected, Mr. Vienna."

But in the sitting room she and Sergeant Lehny were more frank. "Have you seen our publicity?" Jack Lehny swept a pile of newspapers off the couch to make a place for Mary. "Good reviews. Front page."

The nurse was shocked. "The 'Daily News' says she'll be scarred for life."

"What life?" the Sergeant asked grimly. "She's a mess."

Fennelley's assistant was a huge young man with black curly hair and cherubic expression who smoked a chubby short-stemmed briar pipe and dressed in country-club tweeds. A master sergeant in the M.P.'s during the war, Lehny considered himself a tough, unsentimental policeman. Fennelley found him insubordinate, imaginative, and impatient of departmental red tape. Ambitious but injudicious. "Say, what is a semilobotomy?"

Mary tried to look severely medicinal. "It's to relieve cerebral pressure. Dr. Lubecke had her on the table for three hours."

Jack nodded toward the bedroom. "Has *he* been here all the time?" In the Sergeant's mind Max was tagged as Suspect No. 1.

"Never left. Even has his meals sent in. Until you came there's been a policeman on the door."

"I'm just relieving. She'll have twenty-four-hour protection from now on."

Moira wondered why Max was not at the directors' meeting. She couldn't find him anywhere but he seemed to be someplace near. Perhaps he was floating overhead. Yes, that was it, he was lying on top of the water looking down at her. The dead man's float. But meanwhile the others were continuing their dignified discussion.

"The key to the situation," the lawyer St. Iles said, "is Max's will. I drew up the document myself." St. Iles was wearing striped trousers and a black Homburg. He was keeping abreast of the table by sitting on his enormous brief case and paddling continually. Marvin had slick gray hair and the pupils of his eyes were tiny cash registers, Moira noticed.

"Even though you pretend to be Max's friend," she said accusingly, "I think you have your eye on the main chance."

"That is a farm that belongs to Lizzie Arden," Josie interrupted, "a competitor of mine in the cosmetic field."

"Did you say Lizzie Borden?" Jay asked. "She gave somebody forty whacks. Dead, you know." He was quite drunk.

"I would gladly murder her myself," Josie said, doing a little flutter kick, "but I keep Igor for that sort of thing."

"Did you try last night? Did you send Igor to strangle me?" Moira demanded.

As Igor came forward, dressed in Nijinsky's costume from "Specter of the Rose," Moira wondered how he had managed to borrow it but then remembered his Russian connections. The rose petals peculiarly suited Igor, who was doing entrechats with the greatest of ease. "I would do anything for a dough-lar," he smiled, and showed his magnificent false teeth in a smile. "But murder, no. Of course, we never know until we are faced with a situation. Even though I am a hairdresser, I am a very practical man. I think of my old age."

From above the water Max called to her. "Baby, baby, can you hear me?" Then he said a great many other things she could not make out.

The directors' room was sinking gradually toward the bottom. I will find Roman gold and Spanish treasure at the bottom of the sea, Moira thought, and Ronnie and I will be rich and safe at last. If they would only let me up from this table I would go away and trouble them no more. I would live in the many-chambered Hotel Nautilus. The pain was intense. "Baby, come back. It was all my fault. I'll never leave you again. Moira baby, forgive me. Please try to live." Whose voice was that? And what had happened to Blayne?

The others were still arguing. And the Nates' were suddenly there, Albert and Dora, Max's servants. And Pauley, the colored chauffeur. Pauley wore a visored cap and a maroon loincloth trimmed with black braid. He saluted Moira and said, "Mrs. Ryan, I am your friend. The Nates' don't like you. They are your enemies."

Josie, at the head of the table, was becoming bored. She couldn't get a word in. "Is *no one* going to admit to this crime?"

There was silence around the table; only the lapping of the waves could be heard. Moira was finding it increasingly difficult to breathe underwater and her head kept coming off.

"There have been two crimes," said a man who had not spoken before. It was a knight in cellophane armor who looked like Max. "Since the maid, Ida, was wearing Mrs. Ryan's mink coat and feathered hat and driving her car, it seems safe to assume that she was mistaken for her mistress."

"How did you know about my coat? I haven't told anyone," Moira protested.

"Sh…" the man in armor replied. "What we want are alibis for that knight. That is, Ida's night. Where was everybody?" He frowned sternly at the entire assemblage. Moira rather liked her new defender, but she could see clearly through his armor a mast key to the penthouse, the size of the traditional Key to the City, which the knight was wearing on a ribbon suspended between his legs. How many of them had keys?

"We want your alibis for Ida's night," her champion repeated. "Turn them in at the front desk when you check out." He bowed in a Continental fashion.

"I was drunk," said Jay Ryan.

"I was in bed," said Josie Vienna.

"I was in bed with her," said Igor Torin.

And then a new voice spoke. "I used to go with Ida but my brother broke it up. Said I shouldn't be shacking up with her maid—he's such a big shot." Moira immediately recognized Felix Vienna, although her head had now sunk to the bottom and her body on the directors' table was quite lonely without it. Felix was a larger, cruder version of Max. He was correctly attired in green snakes, which writhed about his body.

"Baby," Max's voice whispered, "you can't die. I love you. Come back to me."

"That will never happen while I live." What was Mamma Vienna doing at the meeting? Moira was too tired to listen to anyone else. But the old lady insisted on speaking. The water was getting very black now and the faces were barely distinguishable. "I know how to hate and how to kill."

"But we have all failed so far." Josie bowed to her mother-in-law. "There are nine ways to skin a cat. The point is to have the feline without fur. It is the mink that matters, not the means."

Then the directors' room went away and there was only darkness and the sea. It rose in towering waves to engulf Moira, and it was blood-red.

"She's hemorrhaging," the doctor said.

Sergeant Lehny took Mr. Vienna out into the hall. The policeman saw that there were tears in the millionaire's eyes. Maybe he didn't do it, Lehny decided. "I tried to find Sebastian Blayne for you but couldn't reach him. He's not at home."

A moment later Dr. Lubecke came out and the eminent plastic surgeon rattled off commands like a field marshal. Nurses, interns, and robed Sisters of Charity flew in all directions, the hospital staff mobilizing itself for action. "Mr. Vienna." The physician paused in the midst of the confusion he had created. "I'm taking her back to surgery. You'd better go along to the sun deck. In the way here."

"I'll stay with you," Lehny said as Max Vienna turned blindly toward the elevator.

Before the stretcher arrived, Mary, the little nurse, was left with Mrs. Ryan for perhaps two minutes. A nun entered. "The doctor wants you, nurse."

The nun had opened the door so quietly without knocking that Mary looked up startled. She had not met Josie Vienna, and so she did not recognize the woman in nun's habit. "I thought he'd gone up to Surgery," she said.

"That's right. He wants you to assist him."

"Me?"

"I'll watch your patient."

A nurse is not accustomed to questioning authority, particularly in an emergency, and to assist the great Dr. Lubecke would be a feather in her white cap.

As Mary ran out the door the nun reached for something concealed in the voluminous folds of her black garments and crossed to the bed. Looking down through the plastic window of the oxygen tent at the bandaged mummy head, she could see only the dying woman's pale eyelids. At that precise instant Moira Ryan's eyes fluttered open. Awakening, the prisoner inside the terrifying tent tried to scream.

CHAPTER SEVEN

Sebastian Blayne had no alibi for the night of the big blizzard, and it was quite late in the day when he awakened to this fact—in his secretary's bed, wearing only his Countess Mara underdrawers. "Where am I?" he murmured, always the ham.

"Where *were* you is more like it," Maggie replied, planting a cup of black coffee on his chest.

But this question was not to be answered for some hours. Mr. Blayne drew a blank when he tried to review the events of the previous evening. The Blue Boar Inn and that very dead cadaver at the morgue and Fennelley in someone's kitchen were all surrounded by a Scotch Mist. "I suppose Simon dropped me off here?" Neddy suggested tentatively.

"You arrived alone on my doorstep," Maggie told him, "shortly before dawn, and announced that you'd come to discuss the case."

"Ah. Did I say anything else significant?"

"Then you said you were sorry it was a secret and you couldn't talk about it. And would I please call some woman."

"Where are my breeches?"

"I've hidden them. You're staying in bed."

"Do you remember the woman's name?"

"No," Maggie lied, "because right after that you developed the drop-deads."

"My conscience," Neddy groaned," is positively *gnawing* at me, but I don't know what about. My virginity is unassailable—I hope?"

"I slept on the couch, sahib."

"But Maggie, I'm hating myself for *something*."

"Two seconds after you walked in here, darling, you fell on your face."

"I don't suppose you'd have a small absinthe frappé on you? That usually turns the trick—one way or the other."

Then the telephone rang, and it was Beppo. His voice was agonized and high, "Ma-gee, where is Nay-dee?" His accent was pronounced in moments of tension. "He has not slept in his bed. He has not telephoned the hotel. And the papers—have you *seen* the headlines?"

"Eighty-eight," Maggie replied in a tone intended to soothe. Eighty-eight was their danger signal. On the floor of the kitchenette was the 'Herald Tribune,' lying just inside the garbage door.

"Eighty-eight what?" Neddy asked.

"Eighty-eight degrees colder." Maggie sounded very convincing. "You know I don't take a morning paper, Beppo. Do tell me the news."

"Ask Beppo to bring over some fresh clothes for me and a razor."

On the other end of the line the Italian valet was stuttering with emotion. "The blonde one was murdered last night—or anyway, almost. They don't expect her to live. She was beaten up, half strangled, and her skull mashed in. Concussion. Fifty-two stitches," Beppo added with a true reporter's feeling for detail.

"That's very interesting," said Maggie.

"*Interesting?*" screamed Beppo.

"Neddy's here," she coughed, "and wants a fresh wardrobe. And you'd better bring along your first-aid kit. He has—"

"Give me the phone," said Neddy, taking it. "I have a vile cold, a hangover, and no toothbrush. Oh, excuse me, Beppo, good morning."

Several hours later Neddy, full of B-1's and phenobarbital, still had not raised his head long enough to read the headlines.

In Maggie's kitchenette with the door closed Beppo and his co-spy took stock of the situation. "Of course, he's in it up to *here*," the valet hissed. "If he asked you to call Moira Ryan at that time of night, it must mean they're—"

"Chummy," Maggie supplied. "And now the afternoon papers say they're looking for the woman who telephoned. That's me. Yesterday I was happy, I had a good job—and tomorrow I might be in prison."

"I will come to the Tombs, dear, and bring you the 'Reader's Digest' and little delicacies."

"Why, Beep, you do care."

On tiptoe Beppo planted a kiss on her forehead. "Now how do we get Neddy out of town? After all, we can't kidnap him."

Maggie looked at Beppo and Beppo looked at Maggie, one of those long, long looks when all that needs to be said is left unsaid. "What have you heard from that great Broadway producer, Syd Alvyn?"

"At present he is feuding with MGM. Our idea won't work."

"Hold on, Beppito. Do you remember that time at Sardi's when we first plotted this little goulash?"

"Hash, that is? Since I have taken out my first naturalization papers I find foreign phrases pretentious."

"You did a divine imitation of Syd Alvyn." Maggie went into the living room and got the phone. "Give me long-distance, please."

"Ma-gee!" Beppo's voice rose to a treble wail. "I'm no actor."

"The hell you aren't." Five minutes later she thrust the receiver into the trembling plump hands of Blayne's valet. "You're on, kid."

It was three o'clock in New York and noon in Beverly Hills when Jerome Lustig emerged from his swimming pool to answer the telephone on the patio extension. While he talked a Filipino boy dried the movie director's prolapsed abdomen and hairy back and placed a grass hat on his head and a lighted cigar in his mouth. "Well, Syd, we are still speaking? I thought I was off your list. So what's on your mind, dolling?"

"Something I wanted to throw your way, Jerry. Something big," Beppo confided in the Alvyn manner, or what he hoped was the Alvyn manner.

"Favors yet? You don't sound like yourself, Syd."

Beppo-Alvyn admitted that he was suffering from a cold, and indeed his brow was moist and feverish.

"You got snow there? We got a summer day here." The director winked at his beautiful young wife, who was lying beside the pool on a citron-yellow cushion.

Beppo-Alvyn began to talk, and he talked fast.

"This comes straight from the horse's mouth, you say? So he would like to see a great picture made of this book before he dies. Mm." Lustig stroked his belly, ruminating.

"What's the name of it?" Mrs. Lustig asked in the whisky whisper that was her trade-mark in public life.

"You will excuse me a moment, Syd? Candace is talking in my other ear." Jerome Lustig covered the phone with his hand. "Something called 'Time's Fool.' Ever hear of it?"

Candace sat up. "*Hear* of it?" she croaked. "It's only a classic. What would he want?"

"Everything—except money."

"*Syd?*" The famous face registered utter disbelief.

"Syd's not in the deal. We would have to contact Sebastian Blayne himself, and he's not interested in running up his income tax."

Candace's gaunt eyes lighted up. "Get it for me."

Lustig waddled closer to his wife. "No, we don't jump so fast." Then, remembering Syd, he uncovered the receiver and spoke again to New York. "Are you there, dolling? Hold everything, I pay for the call. Candace and I, we have a little conference.

"So what's it about?" Lustig gazed unseeing at his wife's dieted and massaged tan legs. "There is a part for you?"

"The girl Melvina is supposed to be Blayne's first wife, I think. It's veddy, veddy British."

"We could maybe give it an American background?" Lustig saw not the legs of his love but an Academy Award standing on the mantel of his ranch-type fireplace.

Moira Ryan's fate and one of the great masterpieces in English prose hung in the balance while a hungry-eyed, twenty-two-year-old girl pondered. "Would Blayne come out here and do the script himself?"

"That's the gimmick. He would come for nothing or anyway peanuts, Syd says, if we hold out the right kind of carrot."

"You could cut the horses," pronounced Miss Candace Carstairs, late of Sioux City, "and the man's career. Make it about me—Melvina—selfish, vain, a touch of nympho—and then I reform at the end."

Lustig shook his head doubtfully. "We'll have an ego problem. If it's Blayne's own story, like Jolson—"

"All right." Candace lifted her shoulders in a six-thousand-dollars-a-week shrug. "So it's his story. We'll do a Jolson-type thing." She lay back on the citron mat. "Only I'm Jolson."

A few seconds later in New York Beppo put down the receiver and burst into tears. "Ma-gee, what have we done?"

❧ ❧ ❧

That same afternoon Sebastian Blayne's secretary bought three airplane tickets for California and a bottle of Pernod. Beppo could make an excellent absinthe frappé with crushed ice and a little gin added.

On their way to the airport Neddy was quite happy. "Jerry sounded most pleasant over the phone. When did I talk to him?"

"Earlier," said Maggie.

"Where are we now?"

"In a taxi," said Maggie.

"Jerry is an excellent producer," Beppo announced.

"So is J. Arthur Rank," Neddy objected.

"But Mr. Rank hasn't offered to make 'Time's Fool,'" Maggie pointed out. "Jerry has."

"Do I detect someone's fine Italian handiwork here?" Blayne was beginning to smell a rat.

"We had a real blizzard last night," Maggie replied, carrying off the non sequitur with the charm of a white rabbit. "Mistinguett loathes snow. She's lucky to be getting away from it all."

"Where is my dear old poodle girl?"

"Misty is already at the airport," Beppo explained. "She's traveling with us by air freight, a special dispensation due to your distinguished reputation as the Great White Father of Letters."

"Arranged by your friend Jerry Lustig." Maggie added the clincher.

"Dear old Jerry," said Blayne, and began to sing "My Buddy," seguing later into "California, Here I Come."

They were in the air over Chicago when a stewardess dropped the bomb in Blayne's lap. "Would you like to see a paper, sir?"

Penthouse Paramour Of Wealthy Hotelman Brutally Beaten

Across the aisle Maggie McMahon nudged Beppo. "Don't look now, but we've lost. He's gone quite pale."

"Miss McMahon!" Blayne's eyes were hard and glittering as black pebbles.

"Yes, Mr. Blayne?" Whenever Neddy employed her last name, Maggie knew what to expect.

"Kindly inform the stewardess that we are getting off here. And send a message to that cinema chap that I have been unavoidably detained—at the Ambassador East."

"Shall I make reservations for three?"

"I am still undecided as to your fate, Miss McMahon, but reserve a suite. Class dismissed."

❧ ❧ ❧

In the eighteenth-century elegance of the Pump Room, Neddy's heart was warmed a little by flaming steaks, Caesar salad, and a telephone brought to his table by a miniature Nubian slave from the South Side clad in satin knee breeches, brocaded coat, and jeweled turban. Blayne had placed a long-distance call for Lieutenant Fennelley as soon as they landed, but it was nearly midnight before the detective could be located—at home in bed.

"Is that you, Simon?"

"Not really. I was asleep." Fennelley sounded cross.

"You won't mind when I tell you I know Moira Ryan."

"Well?"

To Blayne his friend's tone distinctly said, "What of it? The fact that you list Moira Ryan among your acquaintances is of no interest to me."

Neddy had expected an explosion and received a polite belch. "Shall I come back?"

"That's up to you, son."

No questions about his abrupt departure, no encouragement to return. Fennelley would never believe that he had been duped by Maggie and Beppo. Determined not to show his curiosity, Blayne fell into coyness. "You could urge me a little."

"And you could have told me about Ryan the other night. It seems you called her sometime around four a.m. after I left you at the hotel."

"I called Moira?"

"Oh, you don't remember." Simon's sarcasm was heavy-handed. "Then you'll like to know someone's been using your name."

Fennelley had no idea how badly Blayne wanted to know, but Neddy's pride resisted an explanation. "That entire evening is very nebulous to me. I've been quite ill." Blayne went on to describe in dramatic detail his pain, his pills, his chills, his fever and delirium.

The detective was not impressed. "I remember you were getting the sniffles. But this is costing you money, old boy. Have a good long rest in California."

That was the ultimate insult. Fennelley had pushed Neddy into a reclining chair with other retired gentlemen in Pasadena. "Very well, Simon, I don't have to be hit over the head with a brush-off."

The Lieutenant decided he had punished his erstwhile friend long enough. "It's all right this time, chum, but don't lose your memory again. Now, on the Ida angle, I've had some good lab reports. We're looking for someone who shaves and also—"

"Let us say a man, for instance?"

"Not necessarily. Ida had a razor. It had been washed, but not too carefully."

"You mean," Blayne played it straight, "you found bits of hair under the microscope?"

"Exactly. Bits of *black* hair, and Ida was a blonde."

"Beard or armpits?"

"That cannot be determined. Let us presume the latter. We want a dark lady who shaves, likes mushrooms, and can sew."

"Have you talked to Ringling Brothers?"

The Lieutenant held on to his sense of humor and his temper. "Point two: She whipped together a nice snack—scrambled eggs with mushrooms on toast."

"Men have been known to cook. Never mind, go on, the murderer—or Ida Gibbons—ate hearty meal."

"The autopsy disclosed no mushrooms in Ida's stomach. Point three: a spool of brown thread with a needle stuck in it. Now, a needle doesn't present much of a surface, but we've found a pretty good cross section of an egg-shaped whorl that—"

Neddy could contain himself no longer. His laughter burst out, ringing loud and mocking on Fennelley's eardrums in New

York. "I suppose," he said, still choking, "that Ida's fingerprints were different?"

"Quite different," Simon replied in a voice ten degrees below zero.

Too late Neddy realized that he had trod heavily on Simon's tenderest corn. He had profaned the holy rites of laboratory technique. "I know you think I'm taking all this too lightly, Simon, but actually—" How could he make amends? Ridicule, like the Australian boomerang, is a weapon that will return to slay the sender if he is unwary.

Simon's footwork was fast. "But you never take anything seriously, do you, Neddy? Go on to sunny California, sonny, and I'll stick with my microscope." As a policeman Simon Fennelley was no Javert. The mechanics of unraveling the threads of a mystery interested him far more than the persons involved, his moral sense (in terms of society) being somewhat lacking; or perhaps his pity for people was too great. Actually Blayne and Fennelley were perfect collaborators in their complementary functions. The writer was at home with human behavior while the detective was happiest with stains and bits of hair, the chemistry of crime.

Afterward, when he was looking for some mitigating excuse, Blayne blamed everything on Fennelley's attitude, but their conversation was not enough to explain his highhanded decision to meddle with matters in Fennelley's bailiwick. The mischief began that night when Neddy could not sleep and rang up Maggie's room.

It was late and it was cold and Maggie had been dreaming of Hawaiian sands, but she arose, put on some lipstick, grabbed a blanket and a bottle of cognac, and went down the hall to play Scheherazade. "I gather you are livid," she remarked on entering. "You and Charles Boyer have a vein in your forehead that's a dead giveaway. Or is that passion?"

"Maggie, you know that I am displeased with you?"

"Your silence during the past eighteen hours has been, shall I say, poignant."

"Everyone picks up my style. Stick to your own line of persiflage, my girl. What made you do it?"

Maggie blinked her amber-brown eyes and looked demure. "I simply thought you should make that picture, darling."

"You simply thought. I like that."

"Or maybe I've always wanted to see Hollywood and those big red geraniums."

"The old fox can learn some new tricks, I see. Would you like to reinstate yourself in my affections?"

"Suppose I said no. And almost meant it." Maggie had her moments of not liking clever-clever Neddy.

"If you love me at all, my dear, you will call room service and order some champagne."

"A magnum, naturally?" The secretary reached for the phone.

"By all means. We are going to conduct an experiment." Blayne elaborated at length while they waited for the waiter and Maggie was howling with laughter when he finished. "And so I shall try to recapture that state of mind by creating the same conditions, thereby enabling myself to remember."

"Amnesia was never like this," Maggie commented as she poured the pale foaming gold champagne and, to Neddy's careful instructions, added some of the Cognac.

They settled down to work. "Since I still have some of my cold left, Mummy, I shan't have to catch another, do you think?"

Maggie said they could try a dip in Lake Michigan if all else failed. "But we mustn't forget the pills."

"Scientific heroism." Blayne was wearing his quilted black silk robe with a fur collar and looked wonderful. His cheeks were flushed and his eyes merry. "Now, darling," he raised one eyebrow, "while we're killing time—why did you trick me? Give Papa one good reason."

"Maybe I don't like blondes."

"Very flattering." He wagged a forefinger at her. "But it won't wash."

"Neddy—" Maggie sounded very sober. "Don't get rogueish. You're not a young man, doll, and you won't admit it."

The famous playwright sat down abruptly. It was fully a minute before he recovered. "Is my hair piece showing?"

"Please don't have hurty feelings. You're not serious about Moira Ryan?"

"Good God, is *that* what you thought? Be at ease. But I am serious about helping her." Then he uttered a wild yelp. "Maggie! It's coming back. I remember going up to see her that night...."

His secretary rushed to provide him with another drink, but he waved it aside, and with this one gesture Clever Neddy was sent off stage; the man of learning and true insight emerged. "Moira Ryan is a very sick woman," Sebastian Blayne said gravely. "Sick with fear. And that is the most destructive of all diseases. She has undergone a series of 'accidents' that have unnerved her completely. I dare say there have been ghostly goings-on also. Yes, that would fit. They probably want her to think some malevolent force is involved." Blayne was excited by the idea as he paced up and down. "Yes, something terrible and evil is going on there, but I believe it is a very human hand at work. Even more important, I am convinced Moira is not telling me the entire truth. If I am to help her I must know everything she knows, otherwise I cannot put the pieces together correctly. If she forgets or edits any incident, intentionally or otherwise, my mental picture of the murderer will not be accurate psychologically."

"But why would she lie to you?" Maggie asked.

"I don't know, unless she's so accustomed to deceiving herself that she can no longer distinguish between friend and foe."

Only a long time afterward did Blayne realize how close he had come inadvertently to the truth; for the phone rang at that unsuitable moment. The secretary answered it and registered genuine amazement. "It's Max Vienna."

The millionaire hotelman was embarrassed and inarticulate. Blayne helped him. "How is Mrs. Ryan?"

"They think now she will live. Something the doctor cannot account for saved her life. The doctor says it might have been caused by some great shock, but no one can imagine what it might have been. Anyway, when the doctor went into her room only one of the nuns was with her, and Moira seemed about to go into a state of shock, but the hemorrhaging had stopped. She keeps asking for you."

"Mr. Vienna, you must understand that I am in no way a detective, not even a poor facsimile, but if you would like me to come back—"

For a moment Mr. Vienna was speechless because he had been spared the shame of asking.

"When Mrs. Ryan is able to talk, if she will be frank with me, I think I can arrange to protect her from any further trouble."

"Yes. That is what I want."

"Provided, however, that you do not mention our under-standing to Lieutenant Fennelley."

"If you say so."

"I shan't confide in the police—and I may make certain plans that I shan't confide to you."

"Why is that necessary?" Max obviously didn't care for this clause in the contract.

"Because it's the only way I'll play, Mr. Vienna. I make the rules."

"And those are?"

"No questions. No interference."

There was a long pause before Vienna said, "Agreed."

After Blayne had hung up he turned to his secretary with a wicked-little-boy glint in his eye. "Maggie, I want you to listen carefully. I'm going to give you a rather difficult assignment. But you'll get a bonus for it."

"Oh, am I still in your employ, Mr. B.?"

Then Blayne explained his plan. A half hour later he ended by asking casually, "Is all that clear?"

"Horribly."

"Your end of it won't be so bad. Tedious but not particularly dangerous if you follow instructions. The right kind of apartment—and establish your new identity at a couple of neighborhood stores and the corner pub."

"The last shouldn't be difficult."

"Don't be mysterious or different. Get some less flamboyant clothes, don't use four-letter words, and change your hair. Your picture has been in the news too often with me."

"Did you mention the amount of my bonus?"

"And above all, don't get involved with any men. That could be disastrous."

"What about Beppo?"

"I have a job for him elsewhere."

"And you?"

Neddy never looked smugger. "I've thought of a marvelous hideout."

"But how can I reach you?"

"Call your mother. I'll keep in touch with her. Or put an ad in the personals column of the 'Saturday Review of Literature.'"

"I'm scared already," Maggie wailed. "How long will this go on?"

"Until I find the murderer," Blayne answered, "or he finds me."

CHAPTER EIGHT

Nervous and feeling undressed without Maggie and Beppo in attendance, Sebastian Blayne walked down the ramp at La Guardia Field wishing that he had not undertaken this dubious adventure on his own. In the cold light of morning it seemed utterly pointless. Why this compulsion to help Moira Ryan? Only paper plots after this, he swore. The very idea of conducting a man hunt alone created a vacuum in his stomach. Neddy might have talked himself out of the entire affair if Max Vienna had not been waiting at the end of the ramp with his custom-built Derham town car, a chauffeur who drove with swift precision, and a picnic hamper full of thin sandwiches, hot black coffee, and old brandy. All these catered to Blayne's love of princely ease and served to endear Mr. Vienna to him, although he found Max a rather egocentric and somehow false personality.

"Have you spoiled Moira this way?" Neddy inquired, studying the intense fastidious face of the man beside him.

"I like to think so," Max said. "Tell me, Mr. Blayne, don't you agree that women are stupid to want marriage—always marriage?"

Blayne thought of Melvina and Buttons and Kitty and Sheila, and was silent.

Who can ever say how one person sees another? A former night-club entertainer, the wife of a drunken playboy, an ash-blonde babe with a sense of humor—Moira was none of these things to the man who loved her. She was the fair lady in the tower room (he saw the castle standing in a dark and secret wood), destined to be forever captive to his all-possessing passion (pawing steeds, banners, bright armor, swords). Max Vienna would have laughed at the suggestion that he was living emotionally in the Middle Ages, but as a small hungry child in Austria he had fed on the legend of a medieval baron who had kept a beautiful woman imprisoned in his castle. Only servants saw her face. The baron, so the story went, had indulged her every wish—except her desire for freedom. But he could not tell this story to Mr. Blayne when he had forgotten it himself. Moira was the fulfillment of his youngest, oldest dream, but the boy had not dreamed what it would cost the man to accomplish it, to build the castle, lock her in it, his treasure quite separate and apart from his other world of glittering hotels.

"Now, about our financial arrangement—" Max left the question implied.

Blayne recognized that Vienna was not the sort of man who would appreciate something for nothing. And so for want of a better idea, without meaning it at all, he said, "This car rather appeals to me. I've always wanted a Derham."

"It has a built-in refrigerator and bar." Max pressed a button to demonstrate. "And a full-length bed."

"That should be handy on occasion."

"It's all yours."

"You remind me of a friend of mine, but he's a maharajah."

"If there's anything else you want, name it."

"I told you, I want a free hand."

"All I care about is Moira. You find the bastard and bring him to me."

"I won't promise that."

"Very well, his name, then. I'll do the rest." They shook hands on it and then Max picked up the speaking tube. "Pauley, pull over to the curb and stop."

For all his omniscience, Neddy was not prepared for the next thing that happened. The big Negro driver did as he was told and turned off the ignition, and Max Vienna got out. From his wallet he took two fifty-dollar bills, which he handed to Pauley.

"What's this for, Mr. Max?"

"I've given the car to this gentleman here."

"Yes, sir, but what you want me to do with this here money?" The chauffeur held out the hundred dollars. "You got some bet?"

"That's your wages, and a week in advance." He motioned Pauley out of the car. "Want to get up in front with me, Blayne?" The hotel owner slid under the wheel while the colored man in his pearl-gray uniform stood dazed and unbelieving on the curb, still half-smiling and holding the boss's money. He thought it was some kind of joke. Even after the car had disappeared in the traffic he knew they would come back for him, and waited.

He waited until dark.

✤　✤　✤

Later in the day Sebastian Blayne visited Moira at St. Anthony's Hospital attired in blue flannels, pink shirt, black knit tie, and brown oxfords polished to a mahogany perfection. With Mistinguett, an enormous box of flowers, and a bottle of sparkling burgundy, he was a sensation in the hospital corridor. Neddy ignored the policeman on duty and went straight to Moira's bedside, placed the roses in her arms, and said, "You must come back and sing Carmen for us again sometime."

Moira tried to smile, but the stitches made it a grimace. "Roses," she murmured, without much interest. "How sweet." A caplike bandage covered the shaved head. The bruises were fading, but their coloring was still grotesque.

"They won't let me have a mirror. How do I look?"

"Splendid." He went on quickly, "Do you feel like talking?"

"I don't feel like anything. I don't care any more what happens." Her voice was like an exposed nerve. "But I won't go back and live the way I have been, always knowing there'll be another time."

"That's why I'm here."

"You weren't here when I needed you," she answered bitterly.

The little nurse came in. "Excuse me, Mrs. Ryan, but the supervisor says dogs aren't allowed." She turned to Blayne. "What shall I do with it?"

"It?" Blayne inquired with a pained expression. "Are you by any chance referring to my confidante, my Watson, my seeing eye, my dearest friend, Mistinguett?"

"I mean the dog," said the baffled nurse.

"My child, Mistinguett is a very great lady who has traveled on all the seven seas and been entertained by kings. And incidentally, entertained *them*. Be at ease." He waved a lordly hand. "She will not stain these mediocre carpets. I believe Dr. Lubecke is chief of staff here?" The nurse retired in utter confusion as Neddy turned to Moira. "I know your doctor. Lubby is an old bridge partner of mine."

"I wish he'd let me die." Moira closed her eyes. "Max told me he was meeting you at the airport." She waited. "What do you think of him?"

"There's one thing I'm convinced of—he's in love with you. And he'll marry you if he has to."

"It doesn't matter any longer. I'd like to run away to the ends of the earth."

"Have you a spot in mind? Capetown is nice. Or Tahiti."

Annoyed, Moira Ryan opened her eyes. "If you were in my spot you wouldn't be so funny."

"Ah, that's better. We're going to need all that fighting Irish."

"For what?"

"I have a plan."

"It's too late, Neddy."

Blayne rose and looked around for his hat and stick.

"Where are you going?"

"To cancel the arrangements I've made in your behalf and spend the rest of the winter in Bermuda."

Moira began to cry.

"Will you stop acting?"

"I wasn't acting. I have such a terrible feeling of being lost—no place to go—no place I can hide." Her face was twitching. "I won't live with Max ever again."

Neddy raised an eyebrow. "Oh? Then let's get down to business. Have you talked to Lieutenant Fennelley yet?"

"The doctor hasn't wanted me to."

"Good excuse. But you can't use it indefinitely." Blayne went to the foot of Moira's bed and studied her chart. "You're not in bad shape, my dear. Quite able to talk your head off."

"I've nothing to tell the police."

"Well, let's leave it at that for the moment. Have you any intention of being honest with me?

She flushed and changed the subject—to Felix and Ida. "I believe they still saw each other, in spite of Max. They might have had a date the night she was killed. It would explain my coat."

"Did she ask to borrow it?

"No, but I think now that she must have taken it. And someone else returned it."

"Someone else?" Neddy's scalp was prickling.

She nodded. "You remember we both got the impression that someone was watching us? And then your dog pushed open the door, and I forgot to tell you about the mirror."

"What mirror?"

"The one over the bar. It's a two-way affair. In the library next door it's plate glass. You can see through it like a window when the panel's open."

"I love a secret panel," Blayne said. "You think we were being watched?

"There's a little click it makes when the panel slides back." Her hand inside Blayne's was clammy. "That's what I heard. Then after you left I found my coat in the closet."

"Did you examine it?"

"I looked at it, naturally."

"It was just the same? Hadn't been damaged?"

"Not that I could see."

"The fur wasn't torn? No stains?"

"No, it seemed perfectly all right to me."

"Where is your coat now?"

"Still in my closet, I suppose."

"Why haven't you talked to Fennelley and told him all this?"

Moira evaded Blayne's eyes. "You know the worst thing, Neddy. I can't make myself believe it's someone I know."

"Was there nothing about him you could recognize?"

"In the dark?" She whispered as if someone besides Neddy might be listening. "I was in bed. I'd been trying to get you on the phone." Her whole body seemed to tremble. "I know his hands reached for my throat, and I fought him. I must have got free for a second and then tripped in the bedclothes. He held my head down to the floor and struck me over and over again." She beat her clenched fists against her sides and the tears began to roll down her face as she gasped out the last words, reliving the horror.

Before he left the hospital Blayne obtained her agreement to his plan.

One of Lieutenant Fennelley's favorite sports was reading Bernie Brentwood's column, which he considered the most repulsive and inane in print, but Bernie's nightly effusions sometimes provided valuable leads.

Guess who your indefatigable correspondent saw yesterday on the steps of St. Anthony's Hospital? Sebastian Blayne with his famous French poodle, Misty, waiting for a cab at the Pavilion entrance—natch. Just back from a holiday jaunt to Chicago, Mr. Blayne admitted he was leaving immediately for Bermuda to finish a play he has been contemplating for ten years. The most amusing man on two continents, Neddy (to his familiars) had no witticisms to offer and would not comment on the atom bomb....

Gleefully Simon dialed Blayne's private number at the Park Carlton and was answered by the familiar precise voice. After mutual greetings, Fennelley inquired, "Any witticisms to offer, sahib?"

"I shall hang up if you don't control yourself, Simon." Neddy grew silent. He was not in a playful mood.

"So you've been visiting Mrs. Ryan. How is she?"

"Not allowed visitors yet. I just dropped by with some flowers."

Neither of them referred to their long-distance telephone conversation, but both tried circuitously to draw the other out.

"What's all this about your going to Bermuda?"

"It's quite true. I'm off for a rest."

Fennelley did not believe him for a moment.

"I hate to miss out on this Ryan thing," Blayne said wistfully, "but you'll wrap it up in no time. Probably Max, the jealous lover."

"How do you explain Ida?"

"Mistaken identity. He'd been following Moira's car, saw it pull up at a roadhouse, and suspected a rendezvous. A blonde in a mink coat—from a distance they're all the same."

Fennelley's ears stood up. The mink was news to him.

"Then I suppose he went in after her and cornered her in the ladies' room. You know the rest."

"Give me the full treatment on this, Neddy. What happened after he followed her into the john?"

"Can't you see it? He comes in quietly with a knife in his hand. Her back is to the door." The writer was warming to his task. "She turns and recognizes him. He can't very well palm a butcher knife and apologize." Neddy assumed the killer's role. "Terribly sorry, I thought you were someone else. Naturally you won't mention this to anyone, particularly Mrs. Ryan."

"A masterly reconstruction of the crime," Lieutenant Fennelley told him. And as a matter of fact, it was, but neither the skeptical policeman nor the inventive playwright thought so at the time. Blayne was bluffing. He had no idea *who*, but he had guessed *how*. *Why* was another matter.

"Too bad Max Vienna has an alibi for both nights," the Lieutenant pointed out. "As for your jealousy motive, there's nothing doing in that direction. We tried, but couldn't dig up a thing but a lily."

Neddy sighed. "Too bad. There goes my case. Have you talked to the wife? From what I hear, you won't have any lily problem there."

Fennelley set a little trap. "Send me a postcard from Bermuda?"

"Natch."

"When are you sailing, chum?"

"Tomorrow night on the Mariposa."

While they had been talking, Lieutenant Fennelley had scribbled several lines on his note pad. Tearing the top sheet off, he beckoned to Sergeant Lehny. The notation read, "Find out at Park Carlton if Sebastian Blayne is giving up his suite. Check sailing date and passenger list of S.S. Mariposa."

After a touching farewell was said, Simon and his ulcer had several considerations to weigh. Why had Neddy canceled his Hollywood trip in favor of Bermuda? Was the mink coat a slip on his part or a deliberate plant? He was certainly being sly about something. It was time to beware when the charm was turned on like footlights. The old razzle-dazzle. However, Fennelley decided to follow Neddy's little hint regarding Josie Vienna.

❧   ❧   ❧

The moment the detective had left, Josie bolted the door and ran through the apartment to her bedroom. "You can come out now."

The closet opened and Igor Torin emerged from a row of evening dresses. She fell on the bed laughing. By smoothing his rumpled hair, Igor hoped to restore his dignity, but that is not easy for a naked man. "Why did you let him in?"

"How could I refuse?"

"But to knock on your door unannounced—"

"Actually I liked him. He's quite different in his office."

"I suppose you flirted with him?"

"I tried to. Listen, darling, we must make some sense. He questioned me about Ida and Moira, but he isn't onto the hospital thing yet."

"Well, how could he be? Didn't you say the doctor came into the room before you had time to do anything?"

"Yes, but the doctor knows that *something* frightened Moira, and she may say something. I think she recognized me. Of course, I can always say she was delirious, but still we must be careful."

"Does Fennelley suspect anyone in particular?"

"He wanted to take me into his confidence, but I refused to listen," Josie Vienna said mildly. She was not always so gentle with her aristocratic but thick-witted friend. Tonight, however, she wanted something of him.

In her eggplant and fuchsia-pink boudoir, Igor snuggled under the satin pouf and sipped a glass of vodka. "The Lieutenant is becoming too fond of us, I think." She made love to him with knowing hands. "He might drop by again soon with a search warrant. So you will have to get up, my pet. There's a matter we've neglected that you must take care of on your way home." Josie pulled back the bedclothes and reached between the mattress and the springs.

"Suppose I'm not going home," Igor pouted.

She extracted a black nun's habit, folded it neatly, and put it in a suit box. "I would suggest you check this at Grand Central and dispose of the ticket."

The Russian began to dress reluctantly. "Why I am in this sordid little affair I do not know."

"Money is always sordid, Bublichki." She handed him the package. "Now, don't forget and keep this for your drag bag, dear."

A few minutes later, when Igor Torin came out of the Hotel Elysée on East 54th Street with a box under his arm, a drunk across the street lounging on the iron railing in front of Bill's Gay Nineties suddenly sobered up and started toward Park Avenue not far behind Igor.

Sebastian Blayne had been rather pleased with his latest dialogue on the phone with Fennelley. It was only later, much later, that he recalled certain nuances of doubt in Simon's reactions. And he had been considerably relieved to have the detective's confirmation of his own opinion of Max Vienna.

But there was still something disturbing about the man, an indescribable aura that bothered Blayne. How many lives had he lived, how many backs had he broken on his way up the ladder? He must have enemies. Were they getting at him through Moira?

That evening when the two men met for cocktails, in the Park Carlton penthouse, Vienna made good his grand gesture, but he might have been giving away a pack of cigarettes as he tossed a leather key holder across the table to Blayne and said, "Don't forget your car. It's in the garage here."

In spite of his almost royal condescension, Neddy found himself liking Max—but not enough to confide his plan. Instead he decided to elicit some information about the mink coat, saying that Moira was worried about it.

"Why should she be worried?"

"I really couldn't tell you. She simply asked me to have you check on it."

"But I saw her this afternoon. She didn't mention it to me." He led the way to Moira's dressing room and they made a careful search.

The mink, as Sebastian Blayne had feared, was missing.

"Could my house servants—? They quit the other day. An English couple, very reliable. My wife recommended them, as a matter of fact. I can't believe the Nates' would steal anything—if I'm any judge of character." And his tone implied that he was. Then suddenly the hotelman's poise seemed to crumble. "I can't take this too much longer, Blayne. This waiting and being kept in the dark. If I knew what to expect—"

"The less you know, the better. But don't be surprised if I drop out of the picture for a bit."

"Where can I reach you if anything else happens?"

The two men walked down the hall and into the foyer. Blayne rang for the lift. "Don't worry about Moira. With a police guard day and night—"

"For the moment. I wasn't thinking of Moira, but myself." Max was insistent. "I've got to know how to find you."

"That cancels our agreement." Blayne held out the keys to the Derham.

Max's face froze in a hard smile. "O.K., you win."

Blayne waved his Homburg and stepped into the lift. "What I'm doing is for Moira, remember that. I'll get in touch with you."

Meanwhile, in another part of town, the reliable Albert Nates had spent a highly pleasurable afternoon at the corner pub drinking beer and playing the horses. Flushed by a victory in the last race that evened his account with the bookie, Max Vienna's former houseman had even brought home a present for his wife—a pint of gin and a package of Cheese-Its. "How's the old girl?" Bertie patted her broad bottom, but his glow faded with Dora's greeting.

If a dignified fifty-seven-year-old woman weighing 185 pounds, clad in a faded pink chenille wrapper, can resemble an enraged lioness deprived of fresh meat, Dora Nates was it. "We've been had." She spat out the words. "I went over to Papa Kransky's this afternoon to make our payment on the coat, and he's in the clink."

"You're worried about Kransky? That old crook, he. could give us lessons."

"All I can say is you was born slow, Bertie." Dora enunciated deliberately. "The police raided the shop today and grabbed all his stuff."

"So he's a fence. So he's arrested. So what?" Bertie still missed the point.

His wife clenched her fists and pounded the air. "So we've lost our property, that's what. The police took everything down to headquarters," she snarled, "including my mink."

"*Your* mink?" Nates couldn't help saying it, and then made the fatal mistake of laughing.

Dora went for him with her fingernails and clawed his face. Bertie replied with a staggering slap. The pint of Gilbey's got broken and Bertie cut his hand.

Down at Centre Street in a room Lieutenant Fennelley passed many times each day was Moira Ryan's coat, but the beautiful mink lay buried under a pile of nondescript loot tagged "Kransky," the satin lining concealing exact information concerning the assassin's identity.

CHAPTER NINE

IT began on the subway. He could feel it coming, coming, coming, seeping through his veins, crawling like a million carnivorous ants all over him, deliciously taking possession of his body. The glare of lights, the movement of the swaying train, the other bodies packed close to his, the roar of the cars hurtling through the dark subterranean corridors were pain and pleasure wildly mixed. The stations went by like lighted stages where dummies acted death scenes in the Tunnel of Love. Noise! Glorious, rattling, hooting, clanking mount and swell until it splits the ears, the brain.

Yes, split brain, sever, break, and let him out. Out of the cranium he would arise like a vapor, a god, a bodyless being; he would come out new, knowing his own meaning, complete and secure. The noise was wonderful, and the people, the train leaning around curves, the roar. Louder, louder, faster ...

The assassin was sitting on the slick straw subway seat next to the window. He could see his own reflection in the glass and studied his face with affection, knitting his brows, then smiling, then giving a debonair wink. The gray overcoat and battered hat made him look like anyone else when he was dressed for one of his expeditions, when he felt the pain like a scream, the headache starting. They would never find him. Hide, he must hide, let them seek. With the power of the train becoming his own power, the sense of being himself, his absolute self increased.

Why can't I tell them? he thought. Everyone should know. They could all feel like this, but no, they wouldn't understand, they couldn't.

The way it feels like music, great organ music rolling up to the sky, blood beating drums inside you, blood from you running into the earth and around the roots of trees and feeding a forest.

How does God feel? Part of everything and not anything? Nothing, to be nothing and yet possess it all, to be all.

Shout it out—look at me, I know who I am! But you, you who live like animals scurrying underground to reach your caves in the city cliffs, you think you're civilized. Tomorrow you will kill when they say kill. You will drop death on the others like you in their caves. This is the murder of many while I intend to kill only one or two, and these are necessary. You see? There is one among you knows what it all means.

Wait, I will remember. I know and I know but I keep forgetting.

The man whispering to himself was staring down at his right hand, flexing the fingers, clenching and unclenching his fist spasmodically.

If I visualize my shoulder, my elbow, my arm, my wrist, and concentrate, I can detach my hand from my body and it will not be there. I can think it out of being, make it have no feeling, numb. It was the hand that struck, not me.

I did not do that thing, a silver blade buried in fur and flesh, and the blood coming out red, ruby red on the dark fur, and the white face looking so surprised. That was wrong. She was not the one; the hand made a mistake.

Reprove it, punish it, detach it. Never, never do such a bad thing again. What is bad? I know, but I keep forgetting. Naughty hand, Papa spank. No, who can spank the hand of God?

Suddenly the assassin laughed out loud and two passengers near him turned momentarily in his direction, looked with the blank incurious eyes of New Yorkers and saw nothing but a man who might have had one too many and remembered a joke told at some bar. He felt their eyes and grew still, shrinking inside his coat.

They envy me, he thought. They envy me my thoughts. They want to know what I think about, how I can hide in the night without being found, go anywhere and not be known. Invisible.

That was the secret, to remain invisible.

When the train finally came to the end of the line the man in the gray coat got off with the few remaining passengers, his right hand tucked in his pocket, the arm stiff and useless, the fingers frozen around a gun.

It was still early, too early to visit the place he wanted to go. Then he saw a dime store full of yellow light and shining things to buy, full of sweet taffy smells and friendly warm musky bodies and beautiful pink streamers floating from the ceiling like a carnival, and there was music in the air. Wandering up and down the enchanted aisles, he was intoxicated with all he saw. Candy and jewels and flowered aprons, satin ribbons and pearls and painted trays and boxes of pretty toys, glasses, cups, saucers, bright aluminum pans, and balls of copper mesh.

So many, many things, they made him reel, they whirled about him and he was deliriously happy with all the sights and sounds and smells. This was the way life should always be, like a party, with everyone gay and carefree, with streamers and music and chocolate candy. Invisible, unique, untouchable, he strolled from counter to counter helping himself to a green plastic windmill, a string of beads, and a little toy bird. The tired store cop saw him, but it was almost closing time and what was a few cents' loss to a big goddamn syndicated chain? The lousy rich buggers, they should have bunions. Probably some nut.

So fate arranged it that the assassin was not arrested for shoplifting, and he was able to continue to the house where he had an appointment.

The trim smiling colored woman who opened the door might have been a smart secretary, a manicurist, or a housewife, but she was none of these. Emma's voice was amber honey like her skin.

"We been expecting you, Mistuh Man." She addressed most of her customers thus anonymously. "And I think I got what you like this time." She offered to take his overcoat, but he declined, remembering the treasures in his pocket. "Girls like you like's not so easy to find these days, honey." He accepted a cigarette and highball. "Now, you just make yourself to home and I'll be back in a minute." Emma disappeared down the long hall of the redecorated railroad flat.

At the last door Emma knocked softly and entered without waiting. A thin blonde girl in slacks and collegiate brown-and-white saddle oxfords lay on her stomach across the bed reading a true-detective magazine. She rolled over and smiled at Emma. "Are we going to the movies?"

"Now, Louly, you know you got to work." Emma sat on the edge of the bed and stroked her hair.

"You promised me."

"But I got a big john for you, Louly. Might mean twenty, thirty bucks."

"You know him?"

"Yes and no," Emma said. "Got no idea what his right name is. He don't carry no calling card. But he's been here before. Generally stays a while and sleeps a couple days like he's drunk or sick or something. You gotta see him, Louly."

Louly yawned. "I'd rather see Lana Turner."

"You get out of them sloppy-joe clothes and put on something frilly."

The little blonde got up wearily and started to make up her face.

Emma stopped her. "No make-up. This one's queer for only one thing—virgins. The act has to be real good."

"Oh, one of those."

"You're just in from Arkansas, hon. Your pappy tried to lay you when you was fourteen and you ran away."

"For chrissakes, how old am I now?"

"Fifteen—and don't give him a thing but tail, no matter what he offers you, or you'll lose us a customer. Drink with him, tell him your story, but don't get high." She was standing behind Louly's shoulder watching the girl's young unformed face in the dressing-table mirror. "You don't look much more than a baby, sure 'nough," the older woman sighed, despising herself and her profession.

A few minutes later Emma Myers was back in the front room. "All right, Mistuh Man, just you step this way, please."

Louly played it smart. Some of the time she was conscious of being a great actress and wished Billy Rose could see her. Only it went on so long. He didn't drink, but he shelled out for a bottle of Scotch like a gentleman. And he didn't paw her at first. He didn't even take off his overcoat and gloves. All she had to do was listen to him—something about a dime store and making everyone happy.

Louly wanted to laugh, but Emma told her the act had to be real good. Oh, Jesus, she hated men, the goddamn stallions. And this fool, this one chased her around the room with a string of crappy pearls and tried to bite her.

Finally he caught her, and her body was so small and slender it frightened him to be doing this to a child. But he let the part of him he did not like go on with it while another part was thinking of himself on the subway, that dark passage where the trains shot off like rockets in the dark. Then dimly, from an immeasurable distance, he heard the elevated approaching. The tracks were right outside the window, and the real train became the remembered train. At first he thought of jumping out of the window to stop the terrible noise by thrusting his body in the way, but it would have meant hurting himself and he was not ready for that yet.

He heard the girl's theatrical scream of submission under the roar of the downtown express. It was only a pretense of pain, but it was real to him. His hands wanted to silence her. If he needed a reason, that was it, but his motive was quite different. The one in the toilet and the one in her bedroom and this one in the roaring, rattling dark were all the same. Her choked cries became genuine and terrible. All the time the train was going by he was squeezing her throat. It took so long he couldn't believe there was that much strength in her anemic body, she fought so wildly for survival.

But his fingers won. Then there was nothing for him to do but empty his wallet on the bedside table, take the fantastic wooden bird that had been standing on the table, watching him with its eyes, and leave by the back stairs.

When Emma returned later from a party in Harlem the flat was very quiet. The other girls had gone. Only Louly waited on a rumpled bed, a string of broken beads beneath her body.

The death of an eighteen-year-old call girl working in a house run by a Negro woman who paid for protection was not a subject that the police cared to publicize. Her career as a corpse was as anonymous as her life. Two days later Louly was in the ground and her death forgotten by nearly everyone but Emma Myers, who never talked about it unless she was with people she trusted, like Muley and Keefe and their friend, a white man, who was always drunk.

He rolled over on the bed and let his head hang down toward the floor, where several newspapers were spread to catch the vomit that flowed from his parched mouth.

"Gettin' so you hit it every time, boss." The little Negro man at the other end of the room looked up from his book and spoke in a mild melodious voice.

"I'm not your boss, Keefe, just another lush. You're a gentleman and a scholar." Beneath the three-day-old beard there was a faint smile. The sunken eyes traveled over the mildewed walls, the gas plate and wooden icebox, the deal table, the dresser with a cracked mirror, and returned to the black man in his rocking chair. "Could I have a shot?"

"Sure, son. Never gonna be the one to tell you to stop." Keefe washed the pallid face, replaced the soiled papers with clean ones, and gave his friend a slug of gin.

"Think I can sing tonight?"

"Doubt it. You been out too long, boy."

The white man got up, holding onto the brass bedpost and stared down at the newspapers. He blinked his eyes and tried to focus them. "My wife used to sing."

"That so?"

"Looks like her." He pointed at the paper.

"Yeah?" The Negro did not look up.

"Last thing I remember—tried to see my wife. Got all cleaned up and went downtown. Bad snow that night."

"Yeah?" He had heard all this before.

"Stopped for a few nips to get warmed up. Terrible night. Must have been awful late by the time I got there, and then I didn't go in."

Keefe turned a page and answered automatically. "That so?"

"It was funny." He made it to the dresser and poured a trembling tumbler of Dixie Belle. "I stood there in the alley and watched this guy go in the back way and up the service elevator. I didn't try to stop him, just stood there like a big chump with the snow in my face. How's that for ten-twent-thirt?"

"Sorry, boy, what you say?"

"Never mind me. I got the bigger-bagger butterflies. Only two people in this world ever put up with me. You and Moira."

"That your wife? What you say her name was?"

"Moira. Moira Ryan."

"Pretty name." The colored piano player helped his friend to dress. "Come on, kid, let's hit Muley for a steak. Then maybe you'll feel like giving out with some of that Irish boogie."

Little Keefe wondered if the headlines had made sense to Jay, but this was white man's trouble. Suppose his friend stayed in the alley, suppose he was lying or had forgotten that he went up to the penthouse. The black man did not care one way or the other. Jay had saved his life on a slow freight out of Columbus one drizzly night when Keefe had missed his footing.

On their way to Muley's Club, Moira's former husband dropped behind his friend and disappeared in a pawnshop. Keefe understood that he wanted money for a pint but was ashamed to say so. Left alone, Jay hocked his overcoat. But instead of buying liquor, he redeemed his old army automatic.

Felix Vienna had been away from home for two weeks, but whenever he turned up his mother knew better than to ask questions. The unexplained absences, the people who telephoned without giving their names, the large sums of money he sometimes carried—all of these were forbidden topics, along with Max.

A small-time crook, Felix dealt in juke boxes, which he persuaded certain bars to rent. Actually, if there had been no Max, the younger brother would have been happy bullying his bartenders, breaking the boxes of the opposition, listening to the latest bounce tune, watching the fights on television, betting on the ponies; this was his life and work. But always there was the thought of the penthouse atop the glittering pinnacle of the Park Carlton, symbol of all that Max was and he was not.

It was typical of Felix that he had chosen to have an affair with Moira's maid. This he knew would infuriate his brother. And yet he had once tried to do a favor for Max, a peculiar favor. Or at least he sometimes thought of it in that altruistic light. Afterward he could never quite decide whether he meant to skid or the accident had really been an accident. He had been driving a truck on a hijacking job when he recognized a familiar car on the highway and tailed it. Slippery pavement, a curve, brakes that grabbed ... But all this had happened on a rainy night long ago,

Moira was still alive, and the police were looking for someone who wanted her dead.

Lieutenant Fennelley and Sergeant Lehny had visited Mamma Vienna twice and asked a lot of foolish questions. Never the questions she expected, for Mamma had her own theory about the Penthouse Passion Case, but no one inquired in the right way. Sergeant Lehny had talked to her in awkward G.I. German and Fennelley had wooed her with an imported sausage, but the shrewd old lady had been just as deaf and helpless and stupid.

What did it matter, his favorite food? So it is a big steak with onions and mushrooms. Was he moody and irritable? Yes, sometimes, who isn't? A razor at home? He keeps one, sure. But sew? Felix should sew? God forbid.

Mamma began to chuckle, remembering, and told Felix. But he did not find the questions funny at all.

In a 42nd Street Arcade Pauley Jones slouched along the sidewalk without any apparent goal, but his eyes kept turning in one direction. While he threw baseballs at a shivering seminude girl in a trick bed and watched the moving pictures for a penny, he was casing the shooting gallery across the way. Max Vienna would not have recognized his former neat chauffeur in the worn overalls, leather jacket, and overseas cap the big black boy was wearing.

He played a pin-ball game, had a hot dog and coffee, strolled around to Times Square, and then idly headed back. He was waiting for several customers to gather at the pistol range before he stepped up to the counter. The ducks paraded and the wheels revolved, but no one came. Fearful of hanging around too long, he decided to spend his last sixty-five cents on a movie. That meant he would have to work the hole to get back to Harlem—a subway snatch.

While the horses galloped, galloped, galloped across the endless plains, Pauley's fright of what he must do and his self-pity at being driven to do it turned his bowels to water. No job, no money left, nothing coming in, and Pappy down sick. He couldn't follow the story, thinking only of the way he was going to do the thing and what would happen if he was caught.

When he got out of the movie, the Arcade had caught the late show crowd. The big colored boy saw three well-heeled squares approach the pistol range and fell in behind them. Standing at the end of the counter, he waited while the first man bragged, clowned, and took aim with the chained gun. The owner had to walk to the back of the gallery to count the score. Pauley had intended to wait until they were all watching the last man, but instead seized the moment, whipped a pair of wire clippers out of his pocket, cut the chain attaching the gun to the counter in front of him, and sauntered toward the exit. He was almost in the clear when the cry was raised. Every nerve ached with the desire to run, but he stopped and looked with the others in the direction of the yelling, meanwhile easing the target pistol into a trash container.

But he promised himself that he would go back and get it. Because he could not see the boss without it. Not that he meant to use it, unless.... That part he wouldn't think about. The boss would have to listen to reason, that was all. He'd have to give him a second chance or it would be too bad. You couldn't fire a man for no reason and not even give him a reference. The son-of-a-bitch bastard.

Everywhere Emma Myers went, the colored woman hunted among the eight million faces in New York for one face. Her search became an obsession. She followed strangers on the street and stared at them. One day Keefe happened to show her a newspaper picture of Jay's wife, a very candid shot of Moira and Max in evening dress at the Stork Club. The layout included smudgy and distorted likenesses of Josephine Vienna, Igor Torin, Felix Vienna, Albert Nates, Dora Nates, and even Gladys Scherman.

"Funny," Emma said, "that one looks like someone I know." She put a beige finger on one of the faces. "And yet it doesn't."

"You mean that john?" Keefe noticed the way she was holding her purse under the table.

"Yeah." She tore the page out of the paper and stuffed it in her purse. "Anyway, it's a lead," she said.

"You're crazy," he told her.

"Sure. But there's kind of a resemblance." She stood up suddenly and her red lizard purse fell to the floor.

Her companion reached it first. "You ain't the law or the Lord, Em."

"You might as well give it back, Keefe." She smiled and showed her neat white teeth. "It's not very big, honey, but it'll get the job done." She spoke quietly, but Keefe felt the gooseflesh rise on his arms.

⚜ ⚜ ⚜

The doorbell rang and rang and rang and rang and rang. At first the sound was part of his dreams, but finally the steady repetition forced him to come back a long, long way. A memory flickered. It must have been like this when she was alone in the apartment that night.

The doorbell rang again, and Max asked himself if he were frightened. Then in denial he got up, switched on the light, and went quietly down the hall. Whose thumb was pressed against the white pearl button so insistently?

When he slid the bolt and took the chain off, the ringing stopped. "Who is it?" He decided not to turn the latch until there was an answer. Max waited, thinking of Moira, waited with his ear against the door. Footsteps? Were they going away? Who would disturb him at that hour, and then leave without a word? Was that the lift? He raised his voice and questioned the unknown a second time. "Who is there?"

No answer.

A creeping chill went up his backbone and froze the tendons at the base of his neck. Curiosity insisted that he open the door. Fear advised him to remain as he was, safe behind a stout lock. He waited, sweating.

There was no sound at all.

Then he looked. And the foyer was empty. The private elevator was standing with its golden lattice doors pushed back. There was no light in the lift and he could not see into the interior. Standing in the brightly illuminated foyer, the hotel king was reflected endlessly in its mirrored depths.

To the one watching, hidden in the elevator cage, it seemed there were a thousand wicked Maxes to be punished. But which one was he? Then the gun spat out its steel venom and all of them collapsed to the floor.

CHAPTER TEN

WORKING late in his office that night, Lieutenant Fennelley was eating soda tablets like peanuts as he studied the latest reports on his list of suspects. One item in the Igor Torin file puzzled the detective. "Followed subject with package from Hotel Elysée to his apartment. Somewhere en route package got lost," Fennelley read aloud to his assistant Jack Lehny. "What does our man mean by 'package got lost'? Whoever did this job, remind me to lose him."

"Well, sir," the Sergeant took a deep breath, "it was this way. The subject, Igor, went south on Park Avenue at Fifty-fourth. As he rounded the corner he was out of sight for a couple of minutes. When our man caught up with him, the truth is, sir, the package had disappeared."

"Great work. Go on."

"Well, sir, our man was in a dilemma, whether to hang onto Igor or go back and look for the package. Now, here is the picture. The street department was doing some work that night on the corner of Fifty-fourth. There was a manhole open, and it's my guess that he pitched the package down the—"

"*Your guess?*"

"Down the drain," Lehny finished. "Our man tagged Igor as far as his apartment building, phoned for someone to take over his watch, then went back to Fifty-fourth, but the crew had finished work and—"

"And they'd sewed up the street," Fennelley capped him as the teletype started clicking. It was a field report coming in on

Sebastian Blayne: "Subject checked out of Park Carlton, sent luggage to S.S. Mariposa by taxi driver, dined with friends at the Pierre. Attended new Coward play with same crowd, was heard to remark in lobby: "As playwrights, Oscar Wilde, Somerset Maugham, and Noel Coward have much in common—they are not common enough." No hired double could have dropped that deathless epigram, Simon decided, and looked at his wrist watch. There was still time to see Neddy off.

When the detective arrived at Blayne's stateroom there was a champagne party in hilarious progress. Elsa Maxwell greeted the uninvited guest with a kiss, someone called Pete Petrillo took his hat, and Fennelley found himself jammed in a corner next to the commissioner of police. Blayne introduced them. "Tom, this is a lieutenant in your department. Had me shadowed today. Thinks I'm a suspicious character." He laughed to show Murphy it was a joke. "We're old friends, actually." Then someone began singing "Aloha Oe" in a cracked soprano and Neddy yelled, "Bea, darling, when did you get here?" and dove into the crowd.

It was a marvelous party and Fennelley stayed until the last bugle call. Blayne waved to him from the rail as the gangplank was drawn up. "I won't forget that postcard."

On the pier Simon waved back, and was left without a rejoinder. For Neddy to walk out of the big middle of a murder case was grotesquely out of character and smelled of trickery, but Fennelley had no argument now that he had seen it happen. Seeing is believing. So Fennelley did not pick out another familiar face at the rail, or look for. the rather corny device that the playwright—an old hand at staging exits and entrances—had contrived.

As the Lieutenant drove away from the Cunard docks some intuition urged him to make a check on the situation at St. Anthony's Hospital, where the current crime celebrity, Moira Ryan, still lay recuperating in the Pavilion Wing—that medical paradise of glass brick, steel tubing, rubber tile, and functional fenestration.

The Pavilion was built with a long corridor down the center and a short hall at either end, where the elevators were located. Opposite the central ramp in the main corridor was the supervisor's cubicle. As he got off the elevator on the seventeenth floor, Fennelley waved to the nurse and turned right to N-1-17. In the sitting room of Mrs. Ryan's suite he found Sergeant Lehny on duty, reading "Our Inner Conflicts" by Dr. Karen Horney. "Are you troubled by dilemma problems, Sergeant?" he asked.

The young policeman blushed. "There's something I've been meaning to tell you, Lieutenant. You know those footprints on the penthouse terrace? Well, sir, if you remember, there was a twenty-degree rise in temperature the next day." Jack faltered. "Our man didn't get there in time for those prints. They—"

"Got melted?" Fennelley supplied sweetly.

Sergeant Lehny was saved momentarily by Moira Ryan, who called from the bedroom. "Who's out there, Jack?"

The Lieutenant went in to see her. "Why aren't you asleep?"

"Why aren't you?"

"You seem to be allergic to questions, Mrs. Ryan. Someday I hope you'll change your attitude toward the police." He stood at the foot of her bed, hat in hand, studying the woman. "You're protecting someone."

"I keep telling you, Lieutenant, I don't know who it was. Why should I make enemies by guessing?"

"That's what I keep telling them down at the office, sweetheart, but they don't believe me."

Moira examined her vermilion nails under the bed light. "Would you mind my being terribly, terribly frank?"

"It would be a shock, but try it."

"Visiting hours are from three to four in the afternoon."

"Mm." Simon buttoned his overcoat and started for the door, but there he hesitated and seemed to sniff the air like a watchdog who senses a sound, faint and far off, that is beyond human hearing. "You seem jittery."

"I can't sleep."

"Yet you're terribly, terribly eager for me to hurry up and clear out," he mimicked her. "Aren't you?"

"Sorry, Lieutenant, but you do make me nervous."

He watched her drum a cigarette on the tiny face of her diamond-studded watch. "You might get over those nerves if you'd co-operate with us. The murderer may drop by again, you know, without inquiring about visiting hours."

"Will you kindly get the hell out of here, Fennelley? Or shall I ring for the nurse?"

Fennelley clapped his hat on his head. "O.K., Mrs. Ryan, but you can't spend the rest of your life with a police guard. Good night."

In the dim cork-lined corridor the only pool of light came from the goose-neck lamp on the supervisor's desk, illuminating a neat little sign bearing her name in gold letters: Miss Flora MacDermott. Besides Miss Mac, her cubicle also contained the switchboard, drug cabinet, chart rack, an outside phone, and a rented murder mystery.

The night supervisor nodded good-by to Lieutenant Fennelley as he left. No lights on her board and all was well. She resumed her book. "The private eye was alone in his office drinking Old Forrester and worrying about his fee when a voluptuous black-haired babe entered with a Luger tucked under her left...." Flora MacDermott turned a page. She was Scotch, auburn-headed, thin, practical, thirty-nine years old, and had worked hard all her life. But inside Miss Mac's unawakened breast there beat a passionate heart still eager for impossible adventure and romance.

An hour passed before a man in a brown trench coat, tweed suit, and glasses came up the ramp to the desk. "Could I speak to Mrs. Fowler?" he asked apologetically. "I have a very important message from her husband."

"It's much too late," the nurse said as she studied her floor chart. "I'm sorry, but we have no Mrs. Fowler. Perhaps the desk downstairs gave you the wrong room. I'll check." She lifted a plug toward the switchboard.

"No, don't bother." The professorial little man smiled behind his glasses. "I'll call my friend's apartment. I'm so absent-minded—might be in the wrong hospital."

Miss Mac heard the rising whine of the emergency elevator as the tweedy visitor trotted down the hall toward a phone booth. She returned to her mystery. "The black-haired babe was leaning against him hard, thigh to thigh, her breasts sticking into him, her lips parted and moist, but the Luger was still ..."

A light blinked on her switchboard as the outside phone rang. She put down her book with a sigh and answered the phone. "Pavilion Seventeen."

"Are you Miss MacDermott?" a vibrant masculine voice asked.

She said she was.

"Miss *Flora* MacDermott?" There was warmth and a sort of hungry eagerness in the voice now.

"Yes. What about it?"

With rising excitement the man almost shrieked. "Good, great, wonderful! This is Joe Blair speaking, Miss MacDermott, for the You-Said-It Better Batter Quiz Program."

"Huh?"

"You're on the air, Miss MacDermott. I'm calling you from Hollywood, California. It's three hours earlier out here and we're still having fun! Now we've got a question we want to ask you, Flora—if I may call you Flora—and when you give us the right answer you will win three thousand dollars in cash! *Three thousand!* Genuine! Undeflated! Old-fashioned dollars!"

The nurse's fingers were numb and the telephone receiver sticky with sweat. "Three thousand dollars?" she managed to say.

The emergency elevator stopped at the seventeenth floor. A man in white wheeled a stretcher down the north hall.

"And that's not all, Miss MacDermott—I mean Flora. If you know the title of our Better Batter Tune—have you been listening?"

"I'm afraid not. You see, I—"

"Wait—I'll whistle it for you."

While the announcer whistled off key, she could feel the forty-eight United States of America, parts of Canada, parts of Alaska, ships at sea, and the Hawaiian Islands waiting for her answer. "It sounds like 'Sweetest Little Feller' to me, but I can't—"

"You're right! Almost. Almost, Flora." The voice was making love to her now. "Sweetest little feller, everybody knows—what?"

Miss MacDermott told herself she should be worrying about the lights blinking on her board. Could she be fired for this? There was nothing in the rules that said . . . N-1-17 flashed on.

The voice was crooning now. "Don't know what to call him, but he's—"

Minutes, hours, years slid by in silence while the nurse struggled to think. Her whole being was suspended in the agony of the moment. A private nurse passed and waved. Miss Mac looked through her.

The young policeman from Mrs. Ryan's room came up to her desk. Miss Mac didn't recognize him. "Can you get Dr. Lubecke for me, Mac?"

"Shut up, I've got a chance to win three thousand dollars."

The voice was still wooing her. "Don't know what to call him but he's mighty *what?* Come on, now. No coaching from the audience. Mighty what?"

"Mac, this is important." Lehny stuck a piece of paper under her nose. "It's a release signed by the doctor. See? Patient dismissed. What's his number?"

Flora MacDermott heard herself saying, "Mighty Like a Rose."

"Are you loaded? Give me that phone."

"Marvelous! Absolutely marvelous! Did you hear that, folks? *Now*, if Miss MacDermott can answer the Quiz Question she will win the twelve-cubic-foot refrigerator, a brand-new de luxe sedan, ten thousand cans of Bookies' Ready-Meat Dog Food—"

"The switchboard downstairs wouldn't give out the doctor's number," the Sergeant said. "Against the rules."

"A trip to Nova Scotia—"

"I've got to check with Dr. Lubecke. This may not be on the level."

"A Tiffany wrist watch, a week end at the Waldorf, three—"

"Look, Mac, please! I don't want to give the Lieutenant another beef."

"Alsatian wolf hounds, an electric dishwasher, a Lady Bountiful silver service—"

"Go away," Mac hissed at Lehny.

"And a *lifetime* supply of You-Said-Its own Better Batter!" The voice reached its orgasmatic climax.

"If there's anything phony about it, then it's time to wake up Fennelley."

"Now for the three-thousand-dollar Quiz Question. Are you ready?"

Miss MacDermott gulped. She said she was ready. A small ranch with orange trees floated before her dazzled inward eye.

"Do you read the Bible, Miss MacDermott?"

"Yes," she quavered.

"Do you know who built the Ark?"

"Mac, get off that outside phone," the Sergeant pleaded, "or let me use the switchboard. I tried to call you from Mrs. Ryan's room, but—"

"If you don't scram, Jack Lehny, I'll kill you."

"I tried a couple of times to get you but you didn't answer. Your board's sure busy. Hey, wake up."

"Is that my question? Who built the Ark?" She was weak with relief. The hospital corridor had given way to a Spanish house with a red tile roof. The urgent lights on her switchboard, the patients who waited, the policeman at her elbow, the tweedy man in the phone booth, the emergency elevator, and the stretcher case were all wiped out of her mind by the magic voice of the announcer. She could barely whisper, "Noah?"

"That's right, Miss MacDermott! That's *perfect!* But who was Noah's wife? *That's* your question. What was her name?"

Desperately she turned to Sergeant Lehny. "Who was Noah's wife?"

"Bugs," the Sergeant muttered as he headed for a phone booth.

In the receiver, which Miss MacDermott held clamped to her ear, an absolute silence waited. Her back was turned to the north hall, but it would not have mattered if she had been looking directly at the elevator. She was aware of only one thing, an aching void. A fortune was here at the other end of the line, and the one word, the open-sesame, would not come. Who was Noah's wife? Flora MacDermott's stern Scottish father had made his children read the Bible every day. God, help me, she prayed, but nothing happened. Neither God nor the vibrant voice came to her rescue. She knew the announcer was waiting, the world was waiting. But it was no use, she couldn't think.

The elevator descended with a stretcher patient, an orderly, and the tweedy man, who had finished his call.

"Mrs. Noah?" Miss MacDermott choked as she dropped the receiver. Then with her face buried in her hands she swallowed bitter tears.

Downstairs at the ambulance emergency entrance, an intern was signing the patient out. He filled in the blank after "Discharge Date," then his pen hovered over "Attending Physician." "You say you're Dr. Lubecke's assistant? Haven't seen you around before."

"I'm Dr. Edwards. Why don't you call Dr. Lubecke and verify his signature?"

"O.K." The intern reached for his phone. "Hope you don't mind, Dr. Edwards. I'm new here."

"That's all right, Doctor. Very sensible. Meanwhile, I'll just have a look at my patient." Opening the rear door, the tweedy physician stepped inside the ambulance. The driver started the engine.

"Do you know his number?" the intern asked.

Dr. Edwards stuck his head out. "A private plane's waiting for us at La Guardia. We're taking her to Mayo's." He waved a sad adieu. "Not much hope. Every moment counts. Sorry."

Before the young man could protest, Dr. Edwards had withdrawn his head and slammed the door as the ambulance sped down the driveway.

CHAPTER ELEVEN

INSIDE the curtained ambulance the man who called himself Dr. Edwards held one hand firmly over his frightened patient's mouth until they were outside the hospital gates. His other hand seemed mysteriously busy to Moira, but she could not see in the dark. Then she heard him chuckle and felt something icy pressed against her flesh.

"It's a Stinger," he said.

Moira calmed down, realized she was holding a thermos cup. "Who are you?"

"Probably the world's greatest actor." The dubious doctor switched on a shaded light.

Opposite her was a rather plump and unprepossessing professional man in rimless spectacles, a baggy suit, and brown raincoat. "Neddy!" she gasped.

"How clever of you." He poured a drink for himself from a silver thermos and sat down on the side of her stretcher bed. "How do you like my mousy brown hair-do?"

"I'd never have recognized you. What makes you look so fat?"

"There is a type of undergarment that actors don upon occasion—similar to long underwear with built-in muscles."

"You don't mean you've got on falsies?"

"Theatricals," Blayne pronounced chillingly.

"Let me feel."

"Don't get fresh."

"Oh, Neddy, you're wonderful. I didn't think you'd get back in time to come yourself."

"I came back on the pilot's launch. But tell me how things went at your end. What about the policeman? Did Pete hit him very hard?"

"No, he didn't have to. Sergeant Lehny locked Pete in the closet and went to call the doctor, I guess. Anyway, I let Pete out and the rest was like clockwork."

"I'll tell you the whole story someday when we have more leisure. Abduction is a serious crime, you know." Then Blayne chuckled. "Simon won't find Lubecke easily. Someone sent Lubby two passes to Billy Rose's new Midnite Matinee. You see, I've been to some trouble to arrange all this. Do you think you can stay away from Max?"

"I told you that's all finished."

"He'll try to find you."

Moira took Blayne's right hand and held it between both of hers. "I'll make you a solemn promise, Neddy. No more Max."

Suddenly, as they rounded a corner, the ambulance's siren began to wail. "We're on Park now," Blayne said, peering through the curtains. "I told Pete to blast his way through if traffic got sticky. We have perhaps five minutes—no longer. I have assumed that Lieutenant Fennelley will alert all squad cars immediately to stop any ambulance in the greater New York area. You must remember there will be other efforts made to find you." Blayne's voice ceased abruptly as the ambulance swerved around a sharp corner. The siren died a moment later. They drifted to a silent stop.

Then the rear door of the ambulance was opened from the outside and a soft foreign voice said, "Right on the nose, sir."

Moira could see a quiet residential street, the dim outline of brownstone stoops, a single scrawny elm tree. "Where are we?" she asked.

"Never mind," Blayne said. The man he called Beppo lifted Moira in his arms and carried her three steps to a waiting automobile.

Even in the dark she recognized the car. "But this is Max's Derham," she protested as the Italian servant deposited her on the full-length bed and tucked a fur robe around her legs.

"Not any more," the servant who was not a servant said.

"The bed and refrigerator suggested our present enterprise," Neddy explained, "on the day Mr. Vienna made me a present of his car."

The Derham shot smoothly into gear with Pete Petrillo at the wheel, Blayne and Beppo on folding seats opposite Moira's couch.

Moira was full of questions. Blayne stemmed the flow by handing her another drink from his thermos. "Oh, absolutely— they'll find the ambulance within the hour, but you'll be well on your way to Chicago by then," he remarked calmly.

Moira sat up clutching the unborn-lamb robe to her bosom. "Chicago! In my nightgown?"

"Why not? Pete's an old friend of mine from the cab stand at the Plaza."

The driver did not look around. "Don't be alarmed, lady. I'm sort of a mystical character. Got nothing on my mind but the universe."

"Satisfied? You'll be safe in Maggie's apartment by tomorrow night."

"Who is Maggie?" Moira wanted to know.

Blayne bypassed the larger question by describing his red-headed secretary's part in the thickening plot. "Beppo and I will not be accompanying you very much farther. We have work to do here."

"We," said the valet with importance, "plan to interview the suspects in a strictly unorthodox manner. And you've forgotten, sir, the lady's subterfuge, if apprehended."

From an attaché case that also held the thermos of cocktails Blayne produced a towel and bottle of chloroform. "If you're stopped, play the sleeping beauty, my dear. But don't overdo it. Pete has his instructions."

She nodded. "Where will you be?"

"What you don't know you can't tell, darling. Your disappearance will make you the It Girl of the Week on television. You are not to go anywhere, see anyone, or speak to anyone. Got that?"

"I might as well be dead."

"You will be," Blayne said, "if this doesn't work."

When Sergeant Lehny finally reached Lieutenant Fennelley with the impossible news that Moira Ryan had vanished from St. Anthony's, Simon had several things to do very quickly. It wasn't until five in the morning, after questioning the hall nurse, Miss MacDermott, the intern on duty at the emergency entrance, and Dr. Lubecke, that it occurred to the detective to notify Max Vienna of Moira's disappearance.

What Fennelley saw when he stepped out of the private elevator was murder. Or so he thought. Max Vienna, with a bullet wound in his neck, was lying on the floor of the mirror-lined foyer. Unconscious, but not at all dead. By the time the doctor arrived, Simon had given the millionaire first aid and brandy and found the bullet imbedded in the doorjamb. And for the first time he found he liked the self-made hotelman.

Although deadly pale, Max was able to laugh at himself. "I think I must have fainted from fright," he said. "Don't tell Moira. It's nothing serious."

But he had lost a great deal of blood, the physician pointed out, and he warned against further shock. The detective was advised not to mention the events at the hospital and Max was put to bed with sodium amytal.

In the lift the only clear fingerprints on the button panel and the elevator door belonged to Max Vienna. A smudged thumbprint believed to be the assassin's later proved to be Sebastian

Blayne's. The bullet, peculiarly flattened by the impact with Max's collarbone, Fennelley sent to the ballistics department for examination. He did not speak to Jack Lehny but once. "Would you please phone Dr. Lubecke and ask him how much he charges for an ulcer operation?"

Under sedation Mr. Vienna slept several hours before he was allowed to see a newspaper, at which time his police bodyguard telephoned headquarters. "You told me to watch for any reaction, Lieutenant. Well, the guy's going beserk. Raving around like I don't know what. Like maybe Bellevue. Those white wings should come and get him. Says he's got to talk to somebody called Blayne. That ring a bell?"

Lieutenant Fennelley said it did—a small one. Whereupon he radioed the captain of the S.S. Mariposa to have passenger Sebastian Blayne contact him immediately.

FENNELLEY
HOMICIDE, N.Y.C.P.D.
DELIVERED MESSAGE. PASSENGER DECLINES CONTACT. ADVISE. IS HE DANGEROUS?
GREGORY NAPHIER, CAPTAIN
S.S.MARIPOSA

CAPTAIN NAPHIER
S.S. MARIPOSA
NOT THE WAY YOU MEAN. IS HE TRAVELING INCOGNITO? ANY PARTICULARS APPRECIATED.
FENNELLEY
HOMICIDE, N.Y.C.P.D.

FENNELLEY
HOMICIDE, N.Y.C.P.D.
PASSENGER NOT INCOGNITO BUT INCOMMUNICADO. REMAINED CABIN THROUGHOUT

VOYAGE. ALL PAPERS IN ORDER. ARRIVING TOMORROW.
SHALL I ADVISE AUTHORITIES?
NAPHIER

CAPTAIN NAPHIER
S.S. MARIPOSA
NO. PERMIT DISEMBARKATION. ON YOUR RETURN
NEW YORK WILL APPRECIATE INTERVIEW RE BLAYNE.
THANKS COOPERATION. REGARDS.
FENNELLEY

Simon was no longer vaguely annoyed with Neddy; he was definitely sore. Then, several days later, a postcard arrived from Blayne blandly ignoring his shipboard behavior. The card was a photograph of Neddy on a bicycle wearing white shorts and a grass hat, smiling at a pretty young Negro girl with a basket of flowers. On the back was a neat inscription: "Living in sin. Wish you were here." It was signed "Gauguin."

Meanwhile Blayne and Beppo quietly carried on their business of detection, traveling obscurely by night and the subway, and reading with great appreciation the newspaper accounts of their nefarious labors. "According to Detective Fennelley, in charge of the case, the attack on the hotel magnate seems to have been carried out by the same criminal hand that attempted to murder his paramour, Mrs. Ryan, some weeks ago," Neddy read aloud from the "Daily News" to his valet. "As a result of the Pavilion snatch, the Gibbons murder, and the penthouse shooting, a nation-wide search has been organized to find this triple offender, who, the police allege, may be a dangerous sex maniac although mentally brilliant, as evidenced by the shrewd cunning with which he planned the hospital abduction of the millionaire's intimate friend."

"Fennelley couldn't be serious?" Beppo inquired.

"I am reminded of a Saroyan play," Neddy observed, "written by Sartre. But you, Beppo, and I are Pirandello characters—dangerous sex maniacs, of course—who wander through the plot lost in a hell of non sequiturs." Suddenly he interrupted himself. "By the way, how was Bermuda? Hot?"

"I wasn't there long enough to notice. I dashed in one of those toy taxis from the boat to the airport. Only stopped to mail your postcard." The valet reached in his breast pocket for a pigskin case. "By the way, here's your passport. I felt like a spy the whole time. What would they have done to me?"

"I doubt that the British sense of humor could be depended on in matters of international law. You might have got off with five years." Blayne dismissed the matter.

"Precisely my own conclusion. So I stored up a few memories on the way over with a little brown-eyed thing from Havana. Remembering your admonition about staying in my stateroom, I didn't emerge during the entire voyage. Neither did she. I know I didn't quite obey your orders, but I hope you won't mind."

"Of course I mind," Neddy sighed. "Tell me, did she pull your hair? I once knew a girl from Guatemala who—" The train roared through a station.

Beppo leaned closer to the eminent man of letters. "No, really?"

"Oh, yes, indeed. And she loved it. Which reminds me of Mrs. Ryan in her chemise. A good sport, don't you think?"

"Why not? It's been rather an expensive kidnaping, and you paid the check. On the other hand, you've done nothing for *her*, actually. We've just been acting out a detective story."

Blayne admitted it. "Perhaps they will let me lend a hand with the theatricals in prison. I really must look up the Lindbergh Law and the Mann Act. If Moira is still in love with Max Vienna, we're sunk. She will inevitably go back to him and he will go to the police and you and I will go to China, where there are no extradition agreements as yet."

"We might try Russia," Beppo suggested. "You have some royalties coming to you from Moscow."

Neddy nudged his valet's side. A man with an early edition had just taken the seat ahead. Over his shoulder they read: "Hospital Getaway Ambulance Found. Only Clue Silver Thermos Cup with Initials M.M.B."

CAPTAIN NAPHIER
S.S. MARIPOSA
WAS BLAYNE WITH FRENCH POODLE?
FENNELLEY

FENNELLEY
HOMICIDE, N.Y.C.P.D.
NOT FRENCH. A CUBAN GIRL. REGARDS.
NAPHIER

CHAPTER TWELVE

J osephine's ... There was a chaste sign in lowercase chromium script over the door of Josephine Vienna's Madison Avenue hairdressing establishment and *salon de beauté*. The shop presented a gray and white pseudo-Regency, middle-Dorothy Draper front, an electric-eye door, and a carpet deep and clinging as quicksand.

The girl at the kidney desk in the reception room surveyed the male intruder before her with a receptionist's cold and practiced eye. From the pink perfection of her lips issued a mid-Atlantic accent. "You wanted to see Madame. Vienna?" she asked, and then, like a court chamberlain in the Gilbert and Sullivan tradition, added, *"in person?"*

The man in the trench coat nodded in affirmation.

"On business?"

"Well..." The mild little man pursed his lips and pedantically adjusted his rimless glasses. "It is a matter of scientific interest. I wish to interview Mrs.—pardon me—Madame Vienna for an article I'm writing on aesthetics. I should like to quote her on the psychology of beauty, shall we say?"

The receptionist asked the man, whom she had already tagged as the professor, to wait, and presently he was shown into a small white cage, which lifted him to the private domain of the plump and predatory nymphomaniac known throughout the world of fashion by her cerise jars with a gold scarab crest.

Madame Vienna was seated at a six-foot modern desk equipped with three lavender telephones. "This is not a publicity stunt?"

Putting down his brief case, the professor blinked engagingly and shook hands. "I'm afraid I told your receptionist something of a lie."

Madame Vienna's eyes became glaciers. "Then I suppose you're selling something?"

"Oh, no, not at all. I didn't tell the little lady downstairs the truth because—oh, I suppose I'm a bit old-fashioned in spite of my work. You see," he went on shyly, blinking behind his glasses, "I'm an interviewer from the Columbia Foundation of Social Research. We are compiling material for a treatise on the modern career woman." He cleared his throat. "That is, the sexual aspects of the modern career woman."

Madame Vienna's artfully arched eyebrow went up a notch. "But why do you come to me?"

"We are interviewing only the most outstanding women in all the professions, the arts, crafts, and trades."

The glaciers began to melt perceptibly.

"Now, if you'd care to give me some of the basic autobiographical facts? You understand that your name will not be used and anything you may tell me will remain anonymous. Now, when did you have your first—uh—emotional experience?" the professor asked with a strictly unorthodox smile and pulled up a cerise chair.

Sebastian Blayne's methods of detection were far more diverting than Simon Fennelley's. Simon was a list-maker. His systematic mind liked to arrange data in columns adorned with x's and *'s and ?'s. These notes to himself he filed in various pockets. At the end of a day, when he came home to his one-room studio apartment in the Village, he would begin his peculiar process of correlating the day's accumulated jottings, stacking and reshuffling his notes many times like a hard loser at solitaire.

Felix Vienna
Familiar with Ida's apt. Liked mushrooms.
Beard: dark-hair follicle same type found in
Ida's razor. Fingerprints: egg-shaped. Carried
gun. 3 arrests: holdups, black market; no
convictions.

Nurse—Miss MacDermott
Dismissed from hosp. for carelessness; phony
radio quiz prog. Later rec'd P.O. money order in
plain env., N.Y. postmark. Left immed. for Calif.
Who has tender conscience? $3,000 worth?

Max Vienna
Time when shot? No check on this. After hosp.
getaway? Connection? Poss. ambush to cover
hosp. biz. M.D. says imposs. wound self-inflicted.

Sebastian Blayne
Why traveling without dog? S.B. without
Misty? No! Where is Maggie? Beppo? Check
with friends.

Thermos Cup

Found in ambulance. Called Scotland Yard. Reply: "Special
order hunting flask & thermos set by Albermarle, Ltd., jewelers,
1911, for Lady Melvina Mumford, deceased."

In the back of his brain, the conscientious lieutenant was
increasingly aware of needing Sebastian Blayne and just as
determined not to acknowledge it. Blayne, meanwhile, in
his pursuit of the flowers of evil, found himself in a cul-de-sac
that smelled perpetually of cabbage: Mrs. McMahon's stuffy little
flat in Queens.

The man who had toured India in a private train as the guest
of a maharajah dragged his once pampered body up three flights
of stairs. The lion of literature waited, trembling slightly inside his
sagging, unpressed clothes, afraid to encounter the shanty-Irish

wrath of Maggie's aunt, Mrs. O'Riordan, who had already begun to gossip in the neighborhood about their roomer, the professor. Ashen-faced, he eased open the front door and listened. No deathless drama on the television set? No hillbilly quartets? No yammering females?

His time was running short, Neddy knew, but he was not prepared for the reception that met him as he stepped into the darkness of the McMahon living room. The muzzle of a gun was shoved into his side. Then a light switch clicked.

Beppo was standing behind the door with a nickel-plated Buck Rogers Special. "Put that thing away," Blayne muttered and leaned against the pea-green wallpaper.

The valet took his master's coat and hat. "You came in too quietly. I thought—"

"I know. Where are they?"

"The movies."

"Thank heaven! An unspeakable day buying drinks for that poor benighted soul, Jay Ryan. All very Eugene O'Neill." Blayne listed to the nearest chair and collapsed. "I'm tired of taking Gallop polls and selling kitchen gadgets and pretending to be a bird lover on a park bench."

"I know your methods, sire," Beppo murmured.

Blayne did not hear him. "I've stepped out of my own sphere, made an ass of myself, and arrived exactly nowhere. All that aside, it's been damned uncomfortable. And I miss a certain detective who shall be nameless. Clues—what do I know about clues?"

"There are one hundred and fourteen varieties of tobacco ash," Beppo replied, but Blayne was too tired to snap at the bait.

Simon Fennelley, however, was making a little better progress with his clues. "The man we want for the St. Anthony's haul," he wrote in a new bulletin to himself, "is a man of some means and education, connected with show business, possibly an actor.

Sentimental, quixotic. Is this the same murderer of Ida? Girl in Jamaica? Moira? Max?"

At that moment the doorbell rang. The Lieutenant turned off the lights, took his service revolver, and went softly to greet his unexpected visitor. Leaning against the bell was the huge, curly-haired, pink-cheeked sergeant, who had never come to the studio apartment before. Since the hospital fiasco Fennelley had treated Lehny like three thirds of a ghost. The melted footsteps and the package lost in the sewer had been forgotten, but Noah's wife had ruined a beautiful friendship. "Well, if it isn't our man. Don't tell me you've got one to top Noah?" Simon asked sarcastically, and immediately regretted it. He smiled.

Jack thrust a sheaf of papers into his superior officer's hand. "Brought you this," he said, and turned to go.

"Won't you come in for a minute and have a drink?"

Music filled the firelit room behind Fennelley's shoulder. In robe and slippers and under the influence of Brahms, bourbon, and Prince Albert, Fennelley was not the man Jack knew at headquarters, but he said, "No, thanks."

Simon pushed the unresisting young policeman into a chair, went out to the kitchenette, and came back with fresh highballs. "Now, tell me how you got these photostats."

Hunched down in his overcoat, the younger man scowled. "Been doing some nightwork on my own. I'll be getting out of your hair tomorrow. Griffin has a berth for me on the vice squad."

"We'll talk about your transfer later. How did you figure the car?"

Jack reached for his drink. "That alibi of Vienna's was strictly from nowhere. I figured he must have grabbed a plane out of here, checked into a hotel, and flew back the same day. Wouldn't risk using his own car to follow Ida. That meant a rented job. So after the murder he has to get rid of it. He doesn't want it reported stolen. On the other hand, he doesn't want the boys at the U-Drive-It garage to look him over a second time. So he parks it across the street where they'll find it."

Fennelley studied the photostatic records of a garage on West 42nd Street: the date, mileage, license number, time checked out, time checked in. The last was a blank. Scribbled across the bottom of the page was a note: "Driver sacrificed deposit by not checking car in."

"This signature could be forged just as easily as Lubecke's on the hospital release. And there's no driver's license number," Fennelley said.

Lehny was crestfallen.

"But," Fennelley added, "I think you've nailed him. We'll have to verify his signature, though. Get yourself uptown fast to the Park Carlton. The bookkeeping department should recognize that scrawl, no matter what time of night it is—if it belongs to the boss's brother."

At that moment the phone rang. "Hold it," Fennelley said. "This may be Scotland Yard calling me back. I asked them to check on Lady Melvina Mumford, the original owner of that cup found in the ambulance."

Sergeant Lehny stood awkwardly at the door while Fennelley spoke a few words into the telephone and did a great deal of listening. Then the Lieutenant tenderly placed the receiver in its cradle. A strange expression came over his face as he studied his notation on the phone pad.

"Lady Melvina Mumford," he read, "weighed eighteen and a half stone—about two hundred and sixty pounds. Great judge of horseflesh and liquor. Always carried sandwich kit fitted with silver flask and thermos. Twice married. Died in 1920 from too many double brandies. Her first husband was Edward Sebastian Blayne."

Fennelley gathered up his other notes on the vanishing lady of St. Anthony's and threw them into the fire. "A gentleman of means and some education. Connected with show business," he remarked bitterly, and held his side where the ulcer was eating, this tireless little organism having been alerted for action by the adrenalin set free in Fennelley while he listened to an unknown voice from Scotland Yard.

But the acid in his stomach was nothing to the caustic of betrayal in his mind as he reached again for the phone and rang the switchboard at Centre Street. "Put one of your operators on this right away," he ordered, "if it means calling every McMahon in the book. The one I want has a daughter named Maggie, who works for a man named Blayne. Sebastian Blayne."

Blayne took Misty to her bed in the kitchen, kissed her good night, and went to the back bedroom, which he shared with Beppo. There he sat down cross-legged on Mrs. McMahon's second-best patchwork quilt from the county Cork. "Beppo," he announced, "it has occurred to me that Darwin may have been wrong. It seems to me that the strongest urge we have in life is not the desire to survive through fitness, but to unfit ourselves and escape. Take Moira, for instance. She has lied to us from the start, when she knows that keeping the truth from us is tantamount to digging her own grave."

Beppo yawned. "I wouldn't try to judge the human race by Moira Ryan."

"Oh, she may have her idiosyncrasies, but she's like everyone else in one thing—trying to escape. Dope or dreams, art or artifacts, we're all searching for a way out, a way not to think, not to be awake and aware. And the most desperate escape hatch of all is—"

"The booby hatch."

"You are incurably light-minded. Let me demonstrate. Q.E.D.: We are all looking for escape. Then let us assume the murderer is no exception and work from my original theory. A psychological portrait of the murderer. If the things people do are like the people themselves, would you say that Moira was attacked by a dope addict, a drunkard, an artist, or a scholar?"

"None of them, for my money."

"Very well. We have remaining the pure escapist, the one who runs away from reality, from himself."

"Excellent, Mr. Holmes, but very superficial."

"You think I'm off the track?"

"I think you're out on a limb. How can you possibly say that the murderer was this type or that or the other? You're excluding a million possibilities."

"Well, in spite of your objections I shall take escapism as a springboard."

"Dive in, I'll hold your coat. But first, allow me to say that the Ida Gibbons thing wasn't the whimsical work of a maniac. It was too well planned. Remember the out-of-order sign? His mind was working every second."

"Very well, if his mind was working as you say, if he had a definite plan when he killed Ida, was he also in possession of his faculties when he tried to strangle Moira?"

"I suppose so. I can't believe there's anything wrong with him. He's too slick."

"There is always something wrong with a murderer. Killing is abnormal. Now, over a period of years, Mrs. Ryan has been the victim of several other attacks. Why has he always failed with Moira? Doesn't it seem likely that he didn't really want her dead?"

Beppo was momentarily nonplused. "That's nonsense." He proceeded to attire himself in black satin Russian pajamas trimmed in jade green.

"Precisely. What is nonsense but the non-sane?"

"Give it to me again—slowly." Beppo got into bed, eying Sebastian Blayne sceptically.

"He killed Ida only because he had to, after she recognized him with a knife in his hand. Perhaps he meant to frighten Moira or hurt her but hadn't intended murder. Suppose he followed to the roadhouse, out of some compulsion, the woman he thought was Moira. That fact in itself would indicate a confused or clouded state of mind. I say he had no real awareness of what was happening. He was like a sleepwalker, a dreamer."

"Did you ever see a dream walking into the ladies' room?" Beppo muttered, and rolled over on his side in the embryo position.

"Crime detection is the exercise of noble minds," Blayne replied.

"A comforting rationalization, sire, but you have yet to detect anything but the smell of old Gorganzola in the sun."

The operator at Centre Street called Fennelley after his six hundred and seventy-first try on the McMahon assignment, and Fennelley called the right Mrs. McMahon back. The second time the right Mrs. McMahon was awakened out of a warm bed she was angrier than all of the wrong Mrs. McMahons put together, and was not inclined to chatter. Yes, she had a daughter Maggie. Maggie was out of town. No, she didn't know where. No, she had no idea where Mr. Blayne was. No, she didn't have a dog. Good-by.

But Simon did not believe her. He had heard the sound, faintly traveling over the miles of telephone wire under the East River through the cement caverns that support Manhattan—the sound of a barking dog. A bark that could be the aged Misty's.

Toward dawn Beppo discovered that his bedmate had disappeared. He found Blayne crouched on the floor, his eyes level with the window sill. "There's a car parked down the block," Neddy explained coolly. "Someone in it. Lying doggo watching this flat. Saw his head pop up a moment ago. Only two possibilities. Fennelley or the murderer."

CHAPTER THIRTEEN

IS BLUE BOAR STABBER SEX SLAYER? Doctors Disagree. Well-known psychiatrist explains jealousy motivation of prisoner whose low I.Q. and social maladjustment have made him insecure with women. Popular with other men, the murdered maid...

MICROSCOPE ANALYSIS TRAPS KILLER. Battle of the Beard solved today by laboratory technique....

MAID'S KEY TO PENTHOUSE FOUND IN LOVER'S POCKET.
At the time of his arrest, Ida's alleged killer had in his possession a key that he insisted was given him by the murdered woman for secret meetings in brother's love nest...."

TRUTH OF HOSPITAL GETAWAY.
The disappearance of Moira Ryan from St. Anthony's Hospital was a police move to protect the socialite singer. Mrs. Ryan's whereabouts cannot be revealed at present. She will be an important witness when Felix Vienna comes to trial."

GARAGE MECHANIC IDENTIFIES FELIX as handsome man who rented black sedan from U-Drive-It Agency....

HANDWRITING EXPERTS DISAGREE. One authority claims Felix Vienna's signature on the car rental records is a self-forgery, written by slayer upside down or in a purposely clumsy fashion in order to..."

IDA'S BOY FRIEND OPENS UP TO REPORTERS...ATTITUDE PUZZLES ALIENISTS. Refuses to make a confession, saying only: 'I'll wait for my day in court.'

In his cell Felix Vienna sprawled on his steel bunk surrounded by newspapers. As the days went by he pored over every line pertaining to the case in every paper, mouthing the words slowly on his lips, tasting each one, resentment of his imprisonment melting as his importance in print assumed fantastic proportions.

The photographers, the reporters, the detectives who questioned him, the lawyers for his defense, the public who wrote fan letters, the guards who brought his food, all gave the younger brother of Max Vienna a feeling of being someone. He had some status. At last he was in the big time. Everyone knew who Felix was now. Max was forgotten.

Quite simply he gave himself up to enjoying every moment of it. He wasn't nervous and he wasn't frightened. The more the circumstantial evidence piled up, the more it pleased him; the trial would take a long time. At the end, the very end, he would step forward and reveal his innocence. Let them have their game of cat and mouse. He knew the score. Or anyway, most of the time he knew. When the psychiatrists talked to him they tried to confuse him. They were supposed to help a guy, weren't they? Not mix him up. Not make him unsure of himself.

Sometimes he refused to answer for the fun of it, and sometimes he lied. It amused him to lead his questioners off like bird dogs on a false scent. He even fooled them with his reactions on the lie detector; they were always positive, the needle quivering upward when Moira was mentioned.

The notoriety was meat and drink to him and he hated to think of the day when it all had to stop. The fact that this might be his last on earth did not occur to Felix. He took a sort of artistic pleasure in baffling his antagonists and changed his story many times. He particularly enjoyed his meetings with the psychiatrists, whose interest flattered him enormously—until it began to dawn on him that the doctors considered him a mental case, and his attorneys were arranging for him to take that way out.

At first the idea of madness was an enormous joke, but one day he saw that no one else was laughing. Could a man be crazy and not know it? Could he do something and forget it? He wasn't sure any more. He could remember the Blue Boar Inn and its neon sign and the highway leading to it. He had driven that road a thousand times, but he could not remember following Ida and doing a thing like that to her in the toilet. The more he thought and read about the crime, the more vivid the whole scene became, except for the knife. He was still kidding the doctors; he asked them where he could have picked up the knife. He began looking at people obliquely. He had no alibi. He begged his mother to swear that he was with her at the time of Ida's death. His mother sent a priest to talk to him. A colored woman came to the police voluntarily and made a sworn statement that she had seen Felix Vienna enter the hotel on the night his brother was shot. He could not sleep. A creeping terror invaded his mind. He no longer clowned with his guards or read the papers. He sat mumbling to himself and staring at the wall. Then a day came when he started screaming. But no one let him out. He beat the cell door with his fists until they bled. Tears ran down his face while he pleaded and cried at the top of his voice, trying to make them hear. But no one listened to his protestations of innocence. No one believed him. Not even himself.

Another obscure parish priest in New York City heard about the case and refused to grant absolution unless the person went to the proper authorities. For this confession had inspired horror in the heart of a man who was the regular recipient of all the sins of humanity. The voice had not belonged to any of his familiar flock, he thought as he hastened down the side aisle. Had the accent been assumed as a disguise? He could not place it. The confessor arrived at the door just as some children in his confirmation class entered and surrounded him. Delayed for a few seconds in his pursuit, the priest ran outside the church and stood on the Gothic porch gazing down the stone steps.

The steps were empty.

But there were several people in the street. Which one? Glimpsing only their retreating backs, the confessor wanted to cry out, "Go now, go before it is too late. Go as I admonished you." Then the lights changed, the passing scene instantly rearranged itself, the traffic flowed around the figures he had been watching, and the city swallowed them.

The priest knew what the muffled voice had told him, but he knew without knowing a name. And the confessional keeps its secrets. Jay Ryan knew both the name and the face, but his information was useless. Gin can be as effective a silencer as Rome. A whore-house madam knew the man but not where to find him. The assassin was safe.

❧ ❧ ❧

"Why doesn't Neddy call?" Moira asked irritably, gazing out the window at the forbidden street. "Suppose the papers were right? Suppose Fennelley *does* know where I am?"

"Face-saving," Maggie said, watching the woman she had grown to pity and dislike tap the window sill with long red nails. "I don't know what you're still worried about. Do you think he'll escape from the Tombs?"

"Felix?"

Maggie sighed to indicate her annoyance with stupidity. "Who else?" The two Irish girls were not a happy combination.

Moira gave her jailor a strangely veiled look. "Do you think he's guilty?"

"Looks like it to me." Now, Maggie thought, she'll light another cigarette and disappear into the kitchenette for a drink. Then back and forth, back and forth across the room from the window to the phone.

"Don't flip your lid, Ryan. How's about checkers?"

"No, thanks." Moira lit a cigarette and dropped the match on the floor. "He's a day late already, nearly twenty-four hours late."

"Mah-jongg, cribbage, chess?"

La Ryan refused to answer.

"I know. Some real nasty canasta?"

"Something's gone wrong."

Blayne's secretary became the heroine of a British weekend-house-party play *circa* George V. "Table tennis, anyone?"

"God, you're funny."

Maggie sat down cross-legged on the divan with a pillow on her lap and reached for a deck of cards. "You know you can trust Neddy."

"Would I be here?" Moira started for the kitchen. "I must have been out of my mind. Ha."

"Ha," Maggie replied as the gurgle of the Scotch bottle reached her ears. She shuffled and laid out the cards for a game of solitaire. She had given up counting how many games; after five hundred it had seemed pointless, although she had consistently beaten the house.

"Something's happened to Neddy," Moira repeated. "I can feel it. Why did I ever let him talk me into this? Fly to South America with Ronnie—" Her laugh was rude and mocking. "What would I do in South America with a nine-year-old child?"

"The same thing you've been doing in North America, doubtless."

"You can keep your cheap sarcasm, dear." Furiously she turned on the tall redheaded girl lounging on the couch. "Wait until you have a kid to support."

Maggie threw down her cards. "You do the patter and I'll do the dance." She went into a soft-shoe time step and shuffled off to the kitchen, took a stiff drink, and came back to the living room, mad and sober. "I've been wanting to say this to you for a long time, Ryan. If you don't go away with that kid *now* and make a fresh start, you don't deserve him."

Tears welled into Moira's eyes and she hid her face in her hands. "I want my baby."

Maggie gave her a Kleenex.

"Please call Beppo. I'll be good." Moira wiped her eyes. "I've got this awful feeling something's happened to Ronnie. You know I'm psychic?"

"Really? What's Russia going to do?"

Moira clenched her teeth. "Radio could use you, Miss McMahon."

"Thanks. Let's not be grim. Doesn't help."

"But why aren't they here? Why haven't we heard from Neddy?"

Maggie would not admit that she shared her companion's premonition of disaster, but to appease Moira she promised to call her mother in Queens that evening. Eight o'clock was the hour Blayne had set for any distress calls. While they waited the Scotch dwindled as the tension between the two women grew.

"Felix might have been working for someone else," Moira said suddenly. "I got away from them. That's why they're after Ronnie."

They and what *they* were going to do was an old story to Maggie, who sometimes wondered if *they* existed outside of Moira's imagination.

"Let me call the school?"

"You might as well call the newspapers," Maggie answered without turning her head.

"If I could talk to Max, he might go up to Ashford and see Ronnie."

"That's a great idea. Simply dandy."

"I wouldn't tell him where I am. It wouldn't do any harm just to—"

Maggie led her charge into the bedroom. "Why don't you take a nap, Ryan? Sleep it off."

Moira flung herself face down across the unmade bed. "I hope I never see you again as long as I live."

"Thanks, darling, it's mutual." In spite of her irritation Maggie lingered in the bedroom. "As long as I live." The words echoed in her mind. If Felix was not the murderer ...

"Ryan, look at me."

The dyed brown head remained buried in a pillow.

"Do you remember what you promised Neddy?"

A muffled yes.

"Does that still go?"

"When you leave, would you kindly close the door?"

"I'm not leaving until you give me your word."

Moira sat up, her blue eyes blazing. "All right, you've got it. Now get out," Moira's voice rose hysterically, "and stop tormenting me, or I'll pick up that phone and call every last one of them. I'd rather be dead than shut up here with you any longer."

Praying for patience, Maggie returned to her sentry duty in the living room. Another twenty-four hours like this and they would be tearing each other limb from limb, the redhead knew. If she could have a few minutes of fresh air and a walk around the block... Maggie grabbed her coat and tiptoed toward the door. Careful to make no noise, she fixed the lock from the outside and quietly eased the door closed.

Lying in the dark and disordered bedroom, Moira stared at the brick wall and fire escape of the adjoining building. It was no jump at all, really. She had heard the latch click when Maggie went out and knew this opportunity might not present itself again. The time had come to decide.

The choice was not difficult; in fact, it was within easy reach. There was a telephone extension by the bed. She had only to stretch out her hand and lift the receiver. "I want to place a long-distance call," she told the operator, "to New York City." She gave the number.

While she waited for the connection Moira opened the window, made sure she could reach the fire escape, and counted the money in Maggie's purse.

CHAPTER FOURTEEN

I t had begun at the station, the sensation that someone was staring at his back. Had that same someone been with him on the train? Blayne wondered. Surely no one connected with the Ryan case had business in the village of Ashford, Connecticut. And yet, walking with Misty from the station to the inn, he found himself looking back over his shoulder surreptitiously.

At the Colonial Inn, Blayne signed the register, walked up the ancient stairs to his room, ordered a drink, and tried to dismiss the bleak feeling in his middle. In the mirror he viewed with satisfaction the octagonal spectacles with frail gold bows, the dun-colored hair, the nubby tweed suit. He looked like a scholarly missionary who as a youth had worked his way through theological school waiting tables. Then forty years in Portuguese West Africa, Neddy decided, without female companionship. The only one he hadn't fooled so far was Mistinguett. The black eyes worshiped him whatever his costume.

Downstairs the hotel clerk signaled the bellboy. "A double brandy for two-o-six."

A guest who was leaning on the desk looked at the clerk and winked. "Is that the old boy with the dog?"

The bored clerk said, "Uh-huh," and went on sorting the mail.

"Mind if I have a look at your register?"

The clerk swung the book around without replying. There was only one name entered: "Walter Mitty, New York City." Mitty of the many disguises was not known to the curious guest, but the French poodle was.

When Mr. Mitty and his dog emerged from Room 206 the next day, the stranger who had recognized Mistinguett was still there, asleep in the pine-paneled lobby of the Colonial Inn. Or at least he had a newspaper over his face.

Blayne took the path leading from the soccer field through a small wood that separated the school grounds from the highway. The boys from Ashford Military Academy were familiar with every stone and hillock, but to a sedentary writer it was rough going. There were sudden banks to be scrambled over and abrupt little turnings between the trees. But with Misty alongside Neddy felt fairly secure even though an early dusk had overtaken them. Underfoot the path was a shapeless blur. His uneasy thoughts, centered on the boy he had learned to know in the past three days, distracted him from the smaller worry of finding his way.

He had come on a sleeveless errand, Neddy knew now.

The first time he had seen Ronnie quite by chance at the sweetshop, and the next day had mingled with proud parents to watch him play right wing for the fourth form in the soccer tournament. For a drawing-room playwright, an athletic engagement involving small boys required courage beyond the call of duty. However, it was his only chance to scratch an acquaintance with Ronnie. There was no point in approaching Cadet Corporal Ryan through the usual avenues. In the Colonel's office he would be a frozen dummy. "How do you do, Ronnie. I'm a friend of your mother. She'd like you to live with her in South America."

But brownies and a hot fudge sundae had done for the nine-year-old what four Martinis would do for Blayne. "In a couple of years I can be a junior counselor at camp and she won't have to pay," Ronnie had told him.

"That's similar to a scholarship?"

"Sure. I'll work for it. And then if my grades are O.K.—after I'm a junior—I can wait table. Ebby says I'll be able to make some real money then and I won't have to take anything else from them."

"Them?"

"Don't you know Max?" Ronnie asked with a simplicity that Blayne thought was the ultimate in sophistication. This brown-eyed boy with his blond hair clipped in a crew cut, sitting erect as a ramrod in a tight gray uniform trimmed with black braid and corporal's chevrons, knew all the answers.

"Do you miss your mother?" Blayne asked, although he knew it was a stupid question.

"Oh. sure." Ronnie was busy licking the last sticky drops from the bottom of his spoon. "I've been at Ashford since I was six," he offered. "I'm an old boy and an officer—means you get a lot of privileges." The wide brown eyes turned to Blayne. "She wants to take me away?"

"Well, that depends. Do you like it here?"

"Oh, absolutely." Ronnie wet his fingers in his glass and wiped them carefully. "But then, I've never been anyplace else. Ebby says when a boy grows up he doesn't need a mother. You can tell her I'm fine."

Ronnie's last words haunted Blayne as he stumbled through the darkening wood. Ronnie *was* fine; that was the thing Moira wouldn't want to know. He was fine without her.

Mentally writing a check to the Ashford Military Academy for Corporal Ryan's future tuition, Blayne was just wondering if uniforms were included when Misty gave a low warning growl. Someone stood before them barring the path. A still, waiting figure. Blayne called hello but there was no answer. Was it a shadow? A tree trunk? Misty would not go forward and Blayne recognized the fact that he was too old to run. There was no retreat.

Suddenly the creaking of the trees grew very loud as he held his breath and listened. Was there another person listening and watching too? Or only an imagined specter? If he had been followed from the city, this was the follower. He waited. And a tree moved.

Of all places to die. But is there ever a suitable spot? So this is it, my Birnam Wood. Let them say of him (after his own fashion Neddy was whistling in the dark), that his last thought was literary. The one who waited had chosen his place well. Beyond the shadow that was a man, the path crossed a narrow watershed, which spanned a ravine at the side of the highway. There was no way to go around the ravine, no other way across.

An old man's voice quavered, "Who are you?"

The shadow did not answer but it came closer.

"What do you want?"

A twig snapped.

Now Blayne could make out a gray overcoat but no face; there was something over the face. "Speak," he whispered, "or the dog will attack on command."

No voice answered. Hands reached for Misty. The proud poodle leaped snarling at the gray overcoat. But like her master, who had not even a sprint left in him, Mistinguett was quite old—no match for the blow that descended to bloody her curls. The dog's scream brought Neddy back from the wasteland. With blood-boiling fury, he lunged with all his strength at the assassin's throat. As they grappled each other and rolled thrashing upon the ground, he suddenly knew all about this faceless man; not who he was, but what he was. With a shudder of horror that paralyzed his will to struggle, Blayne realized how right he had been. But this was no theoretical argument with Beppo. He was in the senseless grip of hands out of control, hands a sick brain could not stop from dealing death.

A soaking rain fell all night. At the bottom of the ravine the playwright's famous face was pressed in the mud. What a critic had once referred to as "the jaunty eye of the elderly elf" was closed. Over him Mistinguett stood guard. After the assassin, frightened by oncoming voices, had thrown his unconscious victim down the embankment and fled, Misty had managed in spite of her own wound to drag Blayne under a projecting boulder and shield him from the weather with her body. The highway was only a stone's throw up the embankment from where Blayne lay bleeding, but Misty would not leave her idol to summon help, although she barked feebly at the headlights of every passing car.

The first thing Blayne knew was a swaying blackness and distant wailing. As he struggled out of the vertiginous void a familiar voice said, "If you say, 'Where am I?' I stand to win five bucks from Sergeant Lehny. Wake up, Neddy."

Opening his eyes, Blayne saw Fennelley's face quite close but out of focus. "Who am I? That's the real question," he said, and then added vaguely, "Something the matter with me?"

"You're full of morphine. You have abrasions of the throat, numerous lacerations and contusions on your body—but nothing serious."

"Nothing serious?" Neddy whispered hoarsely. "Like two crushed kidneys?"

"I mean, you dear old ham, that you're not dying." Which was true, but Fennelley was purposely underplaying. Neddy was more seriously injured than he had indicated.

Blayne saw that they were in the back seat of a police car careening down the highway at eighty miles an hour with the siren screaming. "My contusions would prefer a more leisurely pace." His voice was like the croaking of a wounded crow. "I suppose I must thank you for saving my life?"

"No."

"Are you vexed with me, Simon?"

Fennelley looked away from Blayne's battered, raw, mud-caked, swollen, blue, green, bloody, and infected face. Never in his most sweet unreasonable dreams of revenge had Simon planned for Neddy to suffer this extremity of discomfort. "It was Misty who saved you. I've had a tail on you for days but he was a little late arriving on the scene this evening, and Misty had you well hidden. We're trying to get her to a vet before it's too late."

At their feet, wrapped in a blanket, was the distinguished poodle, her gray ruff soaked black with blood. With an anguished groan, Neddy bent to lift her in his arms. "Dear old girl, dear old girl."

"Don't," Fennelley said. "She shouldn't be moved."

Patting her gently and murmuring baby talk like a lover, Blayne waited for some response. Misty could not lift her head but managed to blink. The saucy shoebutton eyes were glazed and rolled upward under her lids. "Have you given her anything?"

"A little brandy."

Blayne fell back exhausted as the car cannoned around a curve. "I wish I could say the same. My head is in agony."

"Probably concussion. You shouldn't have leaned over. Sorry I can't offer you Lady Mumford's thermos, but maybe this will do." Fennelley poured a half pint of bourbon down Neddy's throat.

Gasping for breath, the playwright allowed himself to utter the oldest cliché of the theatre. "So you know all?"

"All," the Lieutenant snapped, "except the identity of the murderer. If that's who attacked you."

"You *are* vexed, Simon. I rather think you're glad he attacked me." There was a silence that Fennelley made no attempt to fill. "I suppose I should have taken his fingerprints for you, but I forgot to bring along my kit. Not much of a detective, eh?"

Fennelley ignored the apology, but inwardly gave Neddy a grudging tribute. He's a game old cock, the younger man thought, for all his lah-dee-dah elegance. "Who besides Maggie and Beppo knew about your visit to Ashford?"

"Moira, naturally."

"Naturally, eh?"

"I can feel something coming, Simon. Spare me your heavy-handed humor."

"Well, you're a bit behind the times, Neddy. Your damsel in distress has disappeared again. This time without any Houdini tricks on your part. Maggie called me from Chicago. It seems Moira made a long-distance call to her boy friend yesterday and he hopped a plane from La Guardia—to meet her, I suppose. No reason for us to hold him in New York. And now, after your—" Fennelley grinned at Blayne and imitated the writer's favorite conversational gambit—"after your escapade, shall we say, I'll have to kiss Felix good-by. We didn't give him the week end off from the Tombs to murder you in Ashford. So where do we go from here? Any suggestions?"

CHAPTER FIFTEEN

I f you have known someone for a long time you think of him in certain conditioned channels. Max was the man behind the desk for Moira, the man in bed, the man who wrote the checks. For years she had told herself, I'm the only one who understands what he's all about. But now she realized she had never understood him.

Before the house at Malibu they had never had a chance to be alone together, really alone. This man who brought coffee to her in the morning had become quite another and considerate Max. Like an awkward and inexperienced youth, he was struggling to tell her about himself, to get close to her. Once in the middle of the night she had awakened to realize that his pillow was empty. He was kneeling in the moonlight at the foot of the bed, a rosary in his hands.

Without the trappings of grandeur, without his tailored clothes, bowing employees, and custom-built automobiles, Max was someone else. Someone quite different in blue bathing trunks. Afterward when she tried to remember those days at the beach Moira wondered if it had been the fault of the sea. They had lived so simply, so near to the stars, the sun, the sea, the endless sky. What else could have changed them both?

They breakfasted in bed and made love between cups of coffee, bites of toast and marmalade. They slept naked and wore only shorts in the daytime. Moira made no attempt at keeping house except to change the sheets on the bed, empty the ash trays in the fireplace, and order groceries over the phone. This was the shape of their days—slow passionate days spent monotonously swimming and sun-bathing, drinking and napping, dressing and walking to the inn, and returning to sleep again.

But then a day came when it occurred to Moira that their carefree time was drawing to a close. For no reason she could define, she began to know with sure knowledge that they would never marry. And yet she was equally sure that Max loved her. In his own way, was he saying good-by? Had one part of her mind recognized this? Was that why she had put off unpacking?

This was the day they drew their house in the sand and a wave came along. This was the day she made up her mind quite suddenly to call Neddy long-distance. But suppose he made a rude noise and hung up in her face?

There was nothing about Max and Moira in the papers any more. Ida Gibbons lay forgotten. Felix had not yet come to trial. No one knew where Moira Ryan was or cared.

She put in her call that afternoon while Max was having a nap. There seemed no point in telling him; he would only be annoyed, since the mere mention of Blayne's name was anathema after the Chicago business. Besides, Moira reasoned convincingly with herself, she should apologize and explain, and let Neddy know where she was in case of…

The call went through immediately, Maggie answering the phone without the usual long-distance preamble. Blayne's secretary said she was sorry, but Mr. Blayne was out. Who was calling, please?

Mrs. Ryan's feeling for Miss McMahon had not wavered. Moira immediately gave her voice a nasal whine. "This is the long-distance operator. Will you have Mr. Blayne call Malibu, California, seven-eight-nine-five, when he comes in? Thank you."

When she went back to the teahouse Max was awake. Underneath his silky black eyelashes, he watched her drowsily. On the second finger of her right hand was a small ink stain that had not been there before. "Been writing letters?" he asked, reaching for her hand to kiss it.

There was a pen holder and pad on the telephone table and Moira always doodled when she used the phone.

"I thought I heard you talking to someone."

"Don't be silly." She lay down on the lime-green couch beside him. "I was probably talking to myself. I do that sometimes. I was probably saying, 'Moira, you are a very, very fortunate girl to have Max for a lover.'"

Laughing, he pulled her face down to his. "Happy?"

"Uh-huh."

"Make me know it."

She showed him. And he was convinced.

"You'll never run away from me again?"

"Not this winter," she teased.

"I won't let you," he said, and slipped his hand inside her terry robe.

Later, exhausted by their love-making, she asked him to go swimming without her, wanting to be sure to hear the phone. But it did not ring while he was gone. Toward evening she persuaded him to go down to the inn for some cigarettes and new magazines so that she could ask the operator to check with New York.

While she waited, tapping her painted toes, Moira dreaded the thought of Neddy's anger. Had he completely rejected her? No, Neddy had too much curiosity, he would want to know the score. She waited absently for the little click and the operator's voice.

It was quite some time before Moira began to jiggle the receiver up and down, growing more and more impatient. There was no buzzing sound at all. If Max had taken the car he would be back in five minutes and there would be no time to tell Blayne what she wanted to tell him. Suddenly the cold red-and-white checkerboard tiles chilled Moira's bare feet. She could feel the warmth of many days' sun leave her body. It seemed utter madness for her to be standing there in a former movie star's kitchen trying to get New York, for she was forced to acknowledge what she had somehow known all along, the instrument was quite useless.

"How did you happen to discover the phone was dead?" he asked when he came back with the magazines and cigarettes.

"I was—I was trying to catch you at the inn. I wanted some sleeping pills."

"I don't see how it could have been tampered with." Max patted her hand. "We've been here all the time. Probably just disconnected."

"Try it yourself."

He did. He got no dial tone, no answer. "I'll go down and talk to the real-estate people tomorrow. They might have forgotten to pay the phone bill."

"Tomorrow?" It seemed forever.

"Was there someone you wanted to call?"

It seemed simpler to lie. "No. It's just inconvenient," she told him, and made an excuse to go upstairs.

"You're cross." He kissed her and said he would go right away to find out about the phone—maybe see the real-estate man at his home.

While she was alone Moira began to separate their possessions. She packed her winter clothes in one bag and automatically began to fill another suitcase with the things she would want for the trip back east. Was she really going back? Alone? If these days together were not a honeymoon, the beginning of a life together, then they marked the end.

Sweaters, flannels, blue denims, sport jackets, dinner clothes, town clothes, three coats—why so many things? She wondered who had packed this strange conglomeration for him. Ski pants. Riding breeches.

An idea buzzed at the back of her brain, darting like an elusive fly. When their holiday was over, was he going on somewhere else? His bags were obviously packed for a long journey. In the upstairs bedroom where Moira was working, one light was burning, reflected in the dusty mirror of the dressing table. The furniture was still shrouded. They had not troubled to open the heavy shutters. The room had a damp tomblike smell with moth balls superimposed. Bed, chair, table, dresser, each piece of furniture bore a different burden of clothing. Suits on the bed, shirts on the chair, sweaters and woolens on the table.

The sorting went on systematically. How many overcoats did a man need? Town, country, dress. A handful of Old Pine Safetee Crystals in every pocket. The gray coat was unfamiliar and oddly heavy. Things, so many things, and so much trouble. One glove, a dirty handkerchief, and a little plastic windmill in the left pocket. In the right a crushed pack of cigarettes and a—What was it? A funny-looking toy animal with a long beak and bulging eyes. Oh, yes, I remember now, a Worry Bird—that's what they're called. Silly.

Then, in the last pocket of the gray overcoat, the deep breast pocket inside, she found the gun. Her heart began to lurch like a cripple trying to run. She removed the automatic and stood holding it dumbly, dazed. She saw herself in the dusty mirror with the thing in her hand; the other girl, the one with the staring eyes, looked as if she could use a gun, could protect herself with it, could kill. A good idea. Careful to ignore her thudding heart, Moira turned and walked stiff as a marionette to the bed.

Of course it wasn't Max's coat. She couldn't remember ever having seen it before. It wasn't his sort of coat at all. Should she tell him?

The girl in the looking glass shook her head and suggested hiding the black snub-nosed thing under a pillow.

In the club room of Alcoholics Anonymous Jay Ryan put down the newspaper he had been reading. "How long has this been going on?" he asked, pointing a trembling finger at a picture of Felix Vienna.

The big fellow who was Jay's sponsor shrugged. "Coupla months maybe. Why?"

"I know this guy's brother."

"The big hotel shot?"

"Yeah." His nerves were yelling for whisky. "My name's Ryan—or did I tell you?"

The big fellow named Stubby began to laugh. "When we started steaming you out three days ago you didn't know your own—" He stopped and looked at the paper. "*This* Moira Ryan?"

Jay nodded.

"He took her away from you?"

The new convert was honest. "No, a bottle did that." Autobiographical details followed. He told Stubby about the night of the blizzard when he had been hanging around the alley door of the Park Carlton and how later he had even thought of killing Max. "What do you think I should do?"

Jay's sponsor took his A.A. work seriously. "Keep your shirt on, bub. If you want her back, your big problem is to lick the booze. That comes first. If you go to the police now and they fire a lot of questions at you, you'll have a good excuse for a slip. After all, you stayed soused for ten years. It's a little late to start worrying about your wife, isn't it?"

When Max returned she showed him the gray overcoat. He examined the cut and material. "This isn't mine. You know I always have my initials woven in the label."

She showed him the toy windmill and the Worry Bird. "Did you get stinking from drinking, darling, and take the wrong coat from a check stand?"

He shrugged. "I've never seen it before."

"Who packed your bags?"

"I did—in an awful hurry. Remember Chicago?" He hugged her. "I was afraid you'd change your mind."

"But Max, it's very odd you didn't notice," she said lightly. "Someone must have left it in the hall closet—a guest or someone." It was not very convincing but Moira hurried on, determined to explain away the coat. "It could belong to—" Felix, she started to say. But Felix was a subject they mutually avoided. "Lieutenant Fennelley," Moira substituted, and tried to make it sound like a joke.

"Yes," he said seriously, "it could. But I don't think it does. Maybe I'll remember." He picked up the funny little wooden animal with the pop eyes and stood the Worry Bird on his open palm. "I've seen one of these gadgets somewhere before. Notice how the eyes seem to follow you?"

⚜ ⚜ ⚜

"So, in brief, I wish you to instruct me in my duty, Monsignor." The parish priest gazed at the third button on the ecclesiastical vest of his superior and waited for the great man to answer.

The coadjutor bishop disliked making decisions of this nature. "You were her regular confessor?"

"Oh, no. She came to me for the first time a few months ago. From what I could gather—the woman spoke very brokenly—she was afraid her son had committed some crime. He was not like everyone else, she said. My general impression was that these strange seizures she described were, in her mind, peculiar to genius."

"A mother's prejudice."

"Exactly my reaction, Monsignor. But the woman was so distraught I urged her to go to the proper authorities if she had any guilty knowledge of a crime having been committed."

"Quite right, Father. Your hands are clean." The coadjutor bishop was anxious to be done with the matter. The older man

SEBASTIAN BLAYNE

rearranged several papers on his desk to warn of his impatience. Father Gagerty was inclined to be overzealous.

But the little priest gave no indication of rising from the carved uncomfortable chair that the busy executive kept for callers. "The point is, she did not follow my advice. Last night the old lady asked for me and completed her confession. I had no idea who she was until then. The information she had withheld on the first occasion would be extremely valuable to the police, Monsignor. On the night in question—"

"What night?" The senior prelate was by nature precise.

"When the Ryan woman was attacked. The old lady told the police she was not well and awake all night. Therefore, she was able to swear that her son did not leave the house."

"This was an untruth?"

"It seems that he was gone for several hours."

"But we need not leap to the conclusion, Father, that his absence predicates—er—an evil intent." The coadjutor always watered down any statement and added salt.

"If the man is unbalanced, Monsignor—" Lifting his eyes from the black broadcloth vest to the stern face of his superior, the priest experienced a terrible twinge of uncertainty. Perhaps he had been hasty. But Father Gagerty tried once more. "If he is a murderer—" The priest floundered. "After all, the mother is dead."

"To make public her confession, the case would have to be examined by the ecclesiastical authorities, as you know. An apostolic delegate would then dispatch their findings to Rome. If your statements are true, a special dispensation would be necessary. World affairs are very pressing these days. To send a delegate to Rome—" The coadjutor shook his head. "If the woman had not been senile—but old people are inclined to exaggerate." The coadjutor rose. "But of course I'll ask the Bishop's opinion."

The priest likewise rose. "When?"

"As soon as possible, Father, I promise you. The case has not yet come to trial. After all, there's no particular hurry."

Moira opened her eyes and stared at the ceiling after she knew that Max was safely asleep that night. A toy windmill. A Worry Bird. An automatic. What visitor had left them with his gray overcoat in the hall closet of the penthouse? Moira leaned on one elbow and took a sip of beer from a bottle on the floor. Then slowly, cautiously, she lay back on her pillow. Yes, he was asleep. And there was nothing strange about a phone getting out of order. People were constantly having trouble with telephones—otherwise the repair men wouldn't be so busy. Listening to his breathing, she thought, We are like a long dead king and queen, preserved in marble state on their sepulchers, a final mockery of the marriage bed.... Suddenly her limbs went numb. Such an idea would never occur to me, she thought, not in a thousand years. I've never seen a grave like that. A photograph, then? A painting? No. But he might have described it to me. It could be someplace he knew in his childhood. Of course. That's it. Somewhere in Austria, an old church, and he's dreaming about it at the moment. But how does this thought come from him to me?

Something in Moira resisted so violently any sharing of her lover's unconscious that it seemed impossible for the man beside her not to feel her separateness and withdrawal, not to be awakened and warned.

But Max did not stir as inch by inch she slid from the bed and stealthily left the room. Upstairs in the unoccupied bedroom Moira resumed her packing, understanding now that she was getting ready to go away. Before she had been merely putting her things in order in anticipation of their eventual parting. But now she was in a feverish hurry. Was the gun still there? She felt under the pillow. Yes. But something told her to change its hiding place.

Laying out a printed silk dress on the bed, patent-leather sandals, and matching bag, Moira put the gun in her purse with her diamonds and all the money she had. She decided to drive down to the inn and phone from there about tickets and reservations. Or would it be simpler just to get in the car and keep on going to the airport? She wanted to leave quickly now that she had made up her mind. No lingering good-bys, no tears. I will never see him again, she thought—and looked in the mirror of the dressing table to meet his familiar image.

How long had he been standing there naked watching her frantic folding and packing? She had not felt his approach or heard his step on the stairs. His arms reached around her.

##

Emma Myers, the beautiful honey-beige quadroon, fell in love with the new bartender at Muley's place. As it turned out, they had a lot in common. His name was Pauley Jones. Before they were married Emma promised that she would not go back to the racket and Pauley confessed that he had once shot a white man. "I didn't kill the bastard, but I never felt right since. Took precautions, though—didn't want to get no one else in trouble. Roughed the gun up inside the barrel with a file so's they couldn't trace the bullet."

The young Negro, troubled by his conscience, still had moments of wanting to give himself up. But Emma, on discovering the name of Pauley's former employer, stopped him with the story of Louly. Not quite all the story, but enough. "From their pictures in the papers I thought the one I knew was Felix—they look a lot alike. So I went down to this Fennelley's office and gave with the business. But now you make me wonder. The way your boss fired you—" Emma was thoughtful. "I've seen plenty sadists in my line of work. If I've put the wrong john on the spot—"

Pauley held her closer. "We've both been lucky, hon. Don't go bothering round those white men no more. You probably told a mess of lies the first time and you'll get yourself all mixed up in something ain't none of your business. Like my old mammy said—best not stir stale stuff."

Emma lay back in his arms laughing. "All right, doll. You're the boss from now on."

Standing behind Moira with his arms around her waist, Max kissed her back and shoulders. "Going somewhere?" he asked. "I woke up and missed you." He did not add that such a thing had never happened before.

"I couldn't sleep," she said too quickly. "I thought I'd dress and go down to the inn for a drink. It's early yet."

He lounged on the bed, fingering the clothes she had laid out, smoothing the pleated silk dress. "Whatever you'd like."

"I was going to wake you," she went on awkwardly. It all sounded horribly false. In the dressing-table mirror she saw him pick up her bag. "I was beginning to get cabin fever."

"Bored?" His reflection smiled. "Have you forgotten, my darling, why we never go anywhere?"

At his mention of the subject they had long since given up discussing, Moira suddenly saw the patent-leather bag in Max's hand with new eyes. It was the same one she had carried on the afternoon of Ida's death. This was the bag she had dropped running to escape from the unknown man in the garage. She began to remember with terrible clarity how he had held something over the lower part of his face so that only the eyes showed beneath his hat brim. Something oblong and black. Her purse. She had found it on the oily cement floor directly beneath the window of the car where he had stood gazing through the glass at her.

Moira's heart began to protest its fright, throbbing wildly, visibly in her throat. She had never carried that particular purse again, not from that day to this. With any luck it would have the man's fingerprints on it. The only actual evidence of his identity.

"If you still want to go down to the inn, I'd better dress," Max said absently, his attention centered on the bag, which he was cleaning with his handkerchief. "It was all mucky," he added. "I wiped your sandals too."

Their eyes met in the mirror and Moira noticed two things: that Max's smile seemed different now, and that the purse he handed to her was lighter than it had been before.

CHAPTER SIXTEEN

After Mistinguett had been released by the veterinary and Blayne by the hospital, life seemed very unexciting to both poodle and playwright. Beppo was much taken up with playing chess via short-wave radio with Captain Naphier aboard the S.S. Mariposa, and Maggie was in love with a new young man. So it happened one day that Neddy and his reserve champion bitch dropped in unannounced on Lieutenant Fennelley, who had already been assigned to another case, and would have remained there if Neddy had not wandered off that afternoon, bored with waiting for Simon.

Blayne's tour of exploration ended in the vast storeroom where confiscated goods were kept. On a pile of furs labeled "Kransky's Pawnshop" there was a mink coat made of beautifully matched skins that Blayne happened to notice in passing. "This isn't bad," he pointed out to Misty. "Maybe I should buy it for Maggie." As he ran his hand over the soft pelt, his glance fell on the satin lining. There over the pocket were embroidered two initials: M. R. The guard on duty came running at Blayne's whoop of triumph. "I've found the missing mink!"

Where did Max put the keys? Moira asked herself frantically. Get out of the house, that's the important thing. Go down the back stairs quickly while he's dressing. Would the keys be in the car? Keep your legs from shaking, don't trip. Can't run in high heels.

No reason to run. He agreed to go to the inn. You're simply going ahead to start the car. You're perfectly right, he said, we do need a change. Once you're among people in a bright ordinary room you'll feel differently. You'll see then how foolish you've been. He only wiped off your patent-leather purse because it was all mucky. The keys—oh, God, let them be in the car. Be careful of the screen door. Softly. The grass, not the gravel path. Now the garage doors, so dark, hurry, hurry, hurry.

Moira was panting for breath, half sobbing by the time she managed to open the heavy garage doors. Fumbling in the blackness, she felt her way to the car, blindly searched the dashboard, and—oh, blessed relief, the keys were there! She got in, found the starter, and pressed it, but nothing happened; no grinding sound, nothing. A dead battery? Or had the wires been—

Then she saw him.

"M. R. might stand for Mathilda Rasmussen, of course." Blayne made the point before Fennelley could. "But this coat was left at the sign of the three brass balls by one Dora Nates." Attached to the inside pocket was Kransky's tag with the customer's name, number, date, amount of loan, and interest thereon.

The Lieutenant was still not too enthusiastic, but he spread Moira's mink coat on his desk and examined it carefully. "The fur is perfect. If Ida Gibbons was wearing this dandy little six-thousand-dollar job when she was stabbed in the back, why isn't there a rip or gash?"

"Perhaps it's been mended," Blayne offered in defense of his discovery, with which he was overly impressed, in Fennelley's opinion. If Neddy had found marijuana growing unnoticed in a narcotic officer's garden, Simon would have appreciated the joke, but the missing mink in his own back yard was not so funny.

Blayne turned the coat over and peered at the lining. "There's something here. A very faint stain—a sort of water mark—evidently where he washed out the blood."

"The laboratory will answer that." The detective was still disinterested. "I still say you can't plunge a knife through a piece of satin without—"

Blayne interrupted with a sharp exclamation. "Have you a penknife?"

Simon reach in his desk drawer and found an old razor blade. "Anything you need, don't hesitate to mention it. We have all the latest scientific equipment here."

"This bit has been repaired by hand," Blayne continued, deliberately slitting the stitches. "There's no gash because he retailored the lining, making it slightly smaller. Look at the center seam." Neddy laid bare the skins of the little animals who had died to decorate and keep warm the body of Max Vienna's mistress. "Now we know why he stayed so long at Ida's apartment." Beneath the satin and the padding, the answer stared them in the face. "A beautiful job of mending—worthy of a professional furrier," he added with spontaneous admiration. "And I seem to recall that Max was once apprenticed to a furrier."

The Lieutenant's voice rose an octave. "My God—Scotch tape?"

In the middle of the back was a dark circular stain surrounding a two-inch rip in one pelt. The edges of the rip had been deftly fitted together and held with Scotch tape—as neat as a surgical ligature. As the detective bent to examine the evidence he made a strange gurgling noise that Blayne recognized as a chuckle of joy. "Left his signature, Neddy. A magnificent thumbprint where he pressed the tape down." Grabbing the coat, Fennelley headed for the door. "If you want me I'll be in the lab."

"While you're waiting for your report, Simon, I suggest that you get in touch with the Department of Immigration in Washington," Neddy said without the usual Blaynian flourish. A good winner, he was determined to wear his victory laurels lightly. "His prints will be on file there. Max Vienna is a naturalized citizen."

He had been waiting in the garage for her. In the glare of the headlights he stood quite still with something shielding his face. Only the eyes showed, and the eyes were watching her as they had once before. It was the same man.

A gasping horrible sound came from somewhere, like a drowning person makes when struggling for breath. A scream without voice, like a mute utters in terror.

The man she recognized as the murderer came toward her slowly. This time there was no glass between them; the window was rolled down. Moira could not move, could not lift her hand to lock the door. She was paralyzed with fear.

"Please don't scream," he said gently, lowering the purse. "I only meant to show you—it was me."

She could not speak but saw that there were tears in his eyes.

"Will it make any difference, Moira?"

She could not understand. His voice seemed to be coming from a great distance.

"All that's happened—will it make any difference between us?"

Then she heard herself say, "No." Tentatively he touched her shoulder and she did not shrink away from his caress.

"I didn't know how to tell you. I was so afraid you'd run away if you knew."

"I've known for a long time," someone with Moira's voice said, and she realized that it was true.

A messenger from the Department of Immigration delivered the file on Max Koernfeldt to the Federal Bureau of Investigation, where the fingerprints were televised to Lieutenant Fennelley in New York City. Prints of a young alien's hands made many years ago on a pad soaked in purple ink while a long line of tired people waited in a room on Ellis Island. A civil-service employee filled in the government forms and an Austrian boy watched from across the counter. The clerk who rolled the boy's fingers on the pad had seen nothing different about those hands; hands with the golden touch that would amass millions—and strangle and stab....

Fennelley's office was stale with cigarette smoke and the telephone rang every other minute. Mistinguett dozed under Sergeant Lehny's desk while Blayne drank brandy and black coffee from a paper carton.

With his coat off and hair rumpled, Simon lay back almost horizontal in his swivel chair. "It must be late, Neddy."

"I have a book," Blayne answered without raising his eyes from the volume in his lap.

"We're making no progress. You might as well go home."

"Oh, no. Misty and I have settled in for the duration."

"I appreciate your spirit of co-operation, my friend. And I must admit that your experiences as Mr. Tweedy, the inquiring professor, have made you much more plebeian and cozier as a companion, but I am not in the market for a roommate or a Siamese twin. Go home." The Lieutenant's feet hit the floor as a knock came at the door and Maggie entered.

She was looking like a Powers model in a black suit with a leopard muff and beret. "Hi, Si. Excuse the interruption, but it's Neddy's bedtime. I promised the doctor I'd—"

"Don't be dull. The end is in sight." Blayne held up the book he had been reading and waved it under Maggie's nose. "I've been doing a bit of research, and I am now prepared to disclose to your innocent minds exactly the sort of situation we're confronted with here. Or have been confronted with. I imagine all danger is past now. You see—"

"Oh, Neddy, do shut up and come home," Maggie said mildly. "I love you dearly, but you *can* be such a bore sometimes."

"If you are bored, Miss McMahon, I suggest you leave. I, however, intend to tell my friend Fennelley here a few things—of the most extreme interest, by the way—for the good of his soul."

With a sigh Maggie settled into a chair.

"What, still here? Very well, then, but you must both promise not to interrupt me. This is a serious business. Now. Beppo has doubtless told you, Maggie, that for some time I have dallied with the notion that our murderer is an escapist in the extreme sense of the word—a fellow who seeks to escape from unpleasant reality into himself. In my former capacity as a kitchenware salesman I had two very illuminating conversations with Max's mother, and the things she disclosed in no way altered my opinion.

"From Mrs. Vienna I learned that during a family crisis in Max's childhood he left home. That was in Austria after the First World War. Max was the oldest child, and he had been taking care of the other children while his mother worked to support them. When Max decamped, the family was left in a very awkward situation, which he could not have failed to recognize. But Mrs. Vienna told me that after Max grew up and began making money, he provided for her and the rest of the family handsomely. Rather suggests an attempt to salve a guilty conscience on his part, don't you think?"

Blayne did not pause for an answer. "Any psychiatrist can tell you that very strange things can develop from a guilty conscience," he went on. "One of the strangest is called catathymic crisis. I've been refreshing my memory of its details by rereading this excellent book by Dr. Fredric Wertham, an eminent authority. It explains, I believe, what has been going on in Max's disordered mind. In a nutshell, the victim of catathymic crisis conceives the idea that a violent act—against another person or against himself—is the only solution to a profound emotional conflict whose real nature he does not understand.

"Max's several unsuccessful attempts to kill Moira fit into the picture very neatly. Max does not have a basically psychopathic constitution, and so one part of his mind was fiercely resisting his urge toward violence at the same time that the other part of his consciousness was making plans and intending to carry them out. According to Dr. Wertham, the violent climax, when it comes, is a direct result of this inner tension, and usually has no outward provocation at all. The act of violence, you see, is symbolic, and so the killer is unable to think logically about it. Are you following me?"

Maggie merely continued to stare at him with a glazed expression.

Fennelley shrugged. "So Max is crazy. I thought we decided that long ago."

"No, no, no!" Blayne exploded. "You haven't been following at all. I said that Max does *not* have a psychopathic constitution. Catathymic crisis is a mental disorder, but it can hardly be classed with paranoia, for instance. In a sense, it is unique in that it brings with it its own cure. Now, pay attention, children." It was obvious that he was enjoying himself hugely.

"Our killer, having left his family to great distress, over the years built up within himself an unbearable and seemingly unsolvable emotional tension. He blamed this tension, however, entirely on outward events, and his thinking became more and more self-centered. Suddenly he became obsessed with the idea that some violent act was the only way out.

"As is usual in such cases, he struggled against the idea, for he is basically a peaceful man, and of course that only made his inner tension more acute. And so at last he acted."

Blayne paused and picked up the book from which he had been reading earlier. "The esteemed Dr. Wertham says here that after such a violent act has been carried out, the individual loses all of his previous inner tension, and after a while he begins to see that his act was not rational. Looking back on it, he can see that the outer situations of his life did not account for his act of violence, and so it becomes evident to him that his act must have satisfied a deep inner need of which he had not been aware. As soon as he realizes that, of course, he's cured."

Blayne closed the book. "And that's why I believe that Max's violent acts are finished. If Moira told him over the phone that I was up at Ashford, and it could have been no one but Moira, probably his attack on me was purely a protective measure. Either he thought I knew too much, or it was retribution for taking her away from him. But that was a thing apart from his original thinking disorder. The crisis was past. Certainly the times I saw him, he seemed quite normal to me. Superficially normal, perhaps. But judging from the skillful way he arranged his departure, I think the man must be well in control of his faculties. If he has gained insight into his condition and recovered, then I rather doubt we'll ever find him."

On the bed in the shrouded room upstairs, Moira awakened to find Max on his knees beside her, stroking her hair tenderly. "You fainted out in the garage," he said. "And I carried you back to the bedroom in my arms."

She began to see what he wanted. Relinquishing terror, she found the right words on her lips. "The bride was carried over the threshold," she said, and smiled. Like the self-deceiving patient who admits at last that the cancer is there, that the disease is inevitably eating within and the pain will not go away, Moira found a strange sort of release in facing the truth. All that she had fled from was here in this dusty, littered room. She had made this appointment for herself by every choice throughout the years. A rush of memories came—music, perfume, voices. Outside the bridal chamber the sea pounded on the rocks. Would this be the last music she should ever hear?

Max was exhilarated and very gay. "I put some champagne on ice this afternoon. Shall we have a party? I'll get it, if you won't try to run away again."

She shook her head, knowing any further attempt was impossible now. But I must manage to write a note for Ronnie, she thought, and put it in my purse with the diamonds. At least he'll have something.

"We'll make love," her lover said, nuzzling his face against her bare breasts. "Get high on champagne and be mad and bad—before we go."

She did not need to ask where they were going.

"Ah, don't be afraid, baby. I've got to go. You do see that, don't you? And I can't stand it to go alone. But I promise it won't hurt. There'll be only a little minute in between and then I'll be with you always."

CHAPTER SEVENTEEN

"Is that what it says in the book?" Simon's tone implied that books had little or no relation to reality. "O.K. If there's nothing wrong with him, then we can stop worrying about Ryan."

"I didn't say that."

Maggie suddenly pounded the desk and both men jumped. "I've something to tell you both if—"

The telephone stopped her. After a second Simon was beaming at the receiver. "Found the driver? Good. Wonderful. Yes. I see. Discharged passenger at a South Side hotel. Registered under the name of Hadley. Was joined later by his wife, who—"

The rest of Fennelley's conversation was lost on Blayne. At the name of Hadley a low cry from Maggie caught his attention. He saw the blood drain from her face. When Simon had finished with Chicago he found Maggie at his shoulder agog with news. "I was about to tell you a minute ago. Neddy had a long-distance call this morning from California. I thought—"

"Never mind what you thought." Fennelley maintained his usual stoical calm, but his ulcer knew something was up.

"But what I thought is part of it, Si. I didn't really listen to what the operator said because I—I know this sounds weird—had a funny feeling the voice was familiar. Well, it happened so quickly—" Maggie waved her hands in Zasu Pittsian bewilderment. "I can't be sure, but I think it was Moira Ryan."

Fennelley swallowed three white pills. "Why?"

The answer was so obvious, Maggie's shrug said. "She disguised her voice when I answered because she didn't want to talk to me. Maybe that's not logical to a man, but—"

"Not in the least." Fennelley washed down the pills with brandy.

"Anyway, she left a number for Neddy to call." A slip of paper came out of the leopard muff. "When I tried to return the call, Santa Monica reported the number out of order. Later I got another report—that the phone had been disconnected. But the operator gave me the party's name."

Fennelley was leaning forward now, asking for it. "It was Moira Ryan?"

"No," said Maggie.

"Oh, God." Fennelley collapsed.

"The name was Hadley. Mrs. Hadley."

They had their party in the teahouse with the curtains drawn against the sea and the night. A fire blazed on the flagstone hearth and the radio was singing sweetly with a black Carmen's voice. On a low table in front of the couch was their supper, which Max had prepared himself. The food was untouched.

"Cigarette?" He lit one and placed it between her lips.

He didn't offer me the box, she thought. Was this one in his pocket all the time? This could be the way without my knowing. Inhale death.

Max went on talking, the words coming in a flood now that the barrier was gone, the wall of pretending that they were like any other lovers on a holiday. "And then Mother sent me to work. For a butcher. I want you to know these things because they explain why. Why I hated her and tried to make up for it. At the butcher shop I had to wash the blood off the floor and walls. It's one of the first things I can remember—all that blood and the smell of raw meat. They let me have any scraps I found. I'd wash them off and take them home."

Never before in all their years together had he mentioned his childhood. Moira heard his voice only dimly, for she was listening to her own blood speak, urging her to escape, to live, to try once more. There's nothing to lose now, she told herself. It's coming anyway. And dying is only once. But how?

He got up to throw another log on the fire and did not notice that she let her cigarette die in the ash tray. Moira lay on the couch propped up against flowered pillows, the long skirt of her yellow gown spread out in a fan of silk. When he returned to her side Max was careful not to disturb her dress. "You look very beautiful in the firelight." He sat on the edge of the divan and leaned down to kiss her. She held his head against her. "I can hear your heart," he said.

Now? Will it be now? With his hands around my throat? If there were any chance at all ... Watch ....

"My mother was a servant. Did I ever tell you that? She lived in a basement room in a rich man's house. There was only one day a week she could spend at home. So I had to be mother and father both. We were a large family and I was the oldest. Austria was very hungry after the war. The other war. The two smallest died. No doctor would come to us and I couldn't get the right medicine. That's why I ran away. I shouldn't have left them, I know that now. But I was only a kid. I've always felt bad about that. So you see why I had to make money. I thought money was the only thing."

He opened another bottle of champagne. As the cork popped, Moira strangled a cry. Let it be with a gun, not poison, she prayed. The new bottle tasted bitter. Sleeping pills? I asked him to get my prescription filled.

Max stretched out on the couch beside her. "Dearest Moira," he whispered with his lips against her ear. "I promise it will be easy. And I won't spoil your beautiful face. There'll be no scar this time." He held the glass to her mouth and she gulped down the bitter wine. "I want to tell you what happened that night after we quarreled."

Am I getting drowsy? she thought. Or is it only the relief of knowing he will keep me alive to listen to him? Go on talking, Max, go on. Tell me, tell me all of it. Talk until daylight comes. And with it some human being. Someone on the beach I can make hear me.

"The world was so white, all wrapped in white and unreal. Mamma put me to bed and I must have fallen asleep because I think I dreamed this. But all at once I seemed to be standing—the way I used to as a child—at the foot of her bed. I don't know how I got there, but I know that I had it in my mind to do something bad. I didn't think of killing her, really. I just wanted her to be out of the way."

A log in the fireplace crashed and fell apart. The sharp crackling sound brought Max back from the realm of memory. "You're trembling," he said, and took her hands. "I shouldn't be telling you these things. Please believe me, I'm not sick any more or I couldn't talk to you about it. You don't know the way I used to be—so terribly mixed up, like that time at Mamma's. It was the fault of the snow, falling so softly and secretly. It seemed to be saying that whatever I did would be hidden and no one would know. I must have been dreaming, because I remember the blood—it was on my hands from the butcher shop. But it was a sign, don't you see, that I had meant murder. It was clear to me then that not to hurt her, I had to hurt you. It was one or the other. I remember when I got back to the penthouse you were asleep.

"I always wanted you to be asleep so that you wouldn't know me. I guess it was the phone that brought me to my senses. When it rang it upset me and I had to make it stop. I let go of you and then I must have walked out on the terrace to get some air. I knew what I had done. I thought you were dead. And I wanted to cut off my hand. But I had to go back to Mamma's and get some sleep first. I was terribly tired. Later on I punished my hand another way, by making it not there, no part of me."

It was true; he had no feeling in it, she discovered, holding the slender and shapely hand that had driven a knife into Ida's back and strangled the girl Louly between the brass bedposts.

"It's only a trick. I don't do it any more. All that's behind me. I'd really forgotten it—until you found that Worry Bird. You see, there was a girl in Jamaica . . . . Don't be jealous. It didn't mean anything, baby. I remembered her this afternoon when you found that thing. Now that I'm well I know it's ridiculous, but that night in the dark the bird seemed to be watching me with those enormous pop-eyes. I knew it had seen what I did, so I meant to throw it away. But when I got home I hung the coat in the closet and forgot about it."

The teletype clicked out its mechanical message, spacing, punctuating, shifting from line to line with ghostly precision while the operator on the night shift dozed.

attention:
LOS ANGELES POLICE
HOMICIDE DEPARTMENT

REQUEST YOUR CO-OPERATION. URGENT. REPEAT URGENT. MAX VIENNA WANTED HERE FOR MURDER. BELIEVED TO BE IN YOUR AREA.

REFER NEWSPAPER MORGUE CASE OF IDA GIBBONS ET SEQ. VIENNA USING ALIAS OF HADLEY. PROBABLY ACCOMPANIED BY WOMAN MOIRA RYAN UNAWARE OF DANGER.

CHECK ADDRESS 28460 DUME ROAD. COUPLE KNOWN AS HADLEY LIVING THERE RENTED HOUSE. PHONE MALIBU 7895.

UTMOST CAUTION ADVISED. VIENNA PSYCHIATRIC CASE. IF CAN DO SECURE WOMAN BEFORE MAKING ARREST.

AM FLYING WEST COAST LEAVING IMMEDIATELY.

DETECTIVE LIEUTENANT FENNELLEY
N.Y.C.P.D., HOMICIDE DEPARTMENT

"I don't know when I stopped just thinking about it and knew I had to do it. I planned it carefully, just the way I would a business deal. Every detail. In those days I thought so much about killing myself it seemed easy to kill someone else.

"I rented a car in Felix's name and left it at the airport. I went to Pittsburgh, all right, but I came back the same day. That's when I tried in the garage, but it didn't work. So I followed you up to Ashford and back to the roadhouse. But it wasn't you. Ida was going to scream. Poor old girl, she knew who I was. And the little girl in the house that I thought was you screamed too. It was after the thing in Jamaica that I began to feel better. I wasn't troubled any more the way I had been. I can't explain it except to say I felt perfectly all right. Like anybody.

"And I began to see what had been the matter with me. I'd tried all my life to please Mamma and she wanted me to get rid of you. Well, I always had done what she wanted, but with you it was too hard. I was in love with you, but I thought I had to kill you to satisfy Mamma. For years I kept putting it off because you meant so much to me. I tried other times but I didn't really want to hurt you so it never happened right. I knew it was the thing I had to do. If you were alive anywhere in the world I'd want you, so you had to be not alive."

❧ ❧ ❧

On Pacific Coast Highway 101, in front of the Anchor Inn, Squad Car 42, bearing the seal of the California Highway Police, was parked with the engine idling and the radio on low, but Car 42 was empty. The two state troopers were catching a fast cup of coffee before the inn closed.

"Forty-two, Eighteen, or Six—Attention. *Attention. Frantic.*" The radio barked rapid words into the night. "Are you in the Malibu area, Forty-two, Eighteen, or Six? Come in, you bastards, come in. This is *top frantic.*"

Car 18 reported its position near the Ventura county line. Car 6 was twenty miles farther south. Car 42 did not reply.

"I will repeat the message. We are co-operating with the L.A. police. Forty-two, Eighteen, and Six proceed to Two-eight-four-six-o Dume Road. Watch the house until the L.A. boys can get there. Now hear this—it's murder and he's a psycho. So watch it. Car Forty-two, where the hell are you?"

"Jeez," the young state trooper from Squad Car 42 swore under his breath, "it's dark." His companion, according to their plan, would reconnoiter the back of the house, while Joe was supposed to investigate the front and if possible climb to the second story in search of an unlocked window. But it was a moonless night and the sheer smooth walls of the plaster villa defied scaling.

He tried the front door. The knob turned in his hand. The heavy imitation of an Italian Renaissance door opened on oiled hinges and he walked into the house. First he explored the living room, dining room, pantry, and kitchen. No one. The twenty-two-year-old officer helped himself to a bottle of beer, and holding it in his left hand, revolver in his right, proceeded cautiously to the back bedroom. No one. Clothes all over the place but no evidence of a struggle. This psycho sure had some nice suits. Remembering what might be waiting for him at the top of the twisting stairs, Joe decided to have a look around the patio first.

In front of the villa and hidden by it, the little teahouse stood on the beach below the rocks. The radio led him to it. He found a fire burning cheerfully, bubbles ascending in a long-stemmed glass, sandwiches on the coffee table, pillows bearing the imprint of recent use. All these things spoke to Joe in a language he could understand. He could see a man and woman dancing to the radio music, making love in front of the fire. For a moment he lingered in the doorway, his imagination captured by the luxurious setting, the rush of the surf, the passionate violins. But why was the room empty? Someday he would have a place like this. A terrible envy stirred in Joe as the shot rang out.

Racing out of the teahouse onto the beach, he heard screaming that tore the night, an animal kind of screaming that made the sweat run down his legs.

From the chartered plane Sebastian Blayne looked down on the earth, watching the drama of dawn over the Rocky Mountains. The Stage Manager was producing another day. Neddy wondered if Moira Ryan were alive to see it. Fennelley's snore and the drone of the engines finally put him to sleep.

Both men were awakened by the entrance of the copilot into the cabin of the DC-4, which was carrying only the two weary passengers.

"This just arrived, sir." The young man handed a slip of paper to the detective, saluted, and went forward again.

Neddy watched his friend's face—and knew. "Dead?"

Fennelley nodded, still studying the message. "Suicide."

"How?"

"Shot. In the heart."

Remembering the first time he had seen Moira's wide blue eyes, Neddy could not believe they would never lie and flirt and smile again. "I'm surprised she'd take that way out."

"What?" Fennelley raised his voice to compete with the engines.

"Moira. It's not like her," Neddy yelled.

"No. Here, read it yourself."

CHAPTER EIGHTEEN

The mountains look on Malibu and Malibu looks on the sea, and dreaming there one hour alone ... Sebastian Blayne was paraphrasing Lord Byron to suit himself. From his vantage point on a terrace high above the Pacific, Neddy could see the dazzling white shoreline curving leftward to the huddled houses of the colony, on his right the flat top of Point Dume and the mountains in the blue distance. There were other people having tea and cocktails on the deck of the Boathouse Lodge. Blayne, however, ignored their presence while he waited under an umbrella for Moira and Simon Fennelley to come back from town.

For everyone else Max Vienna was dead and buried. Neddy had attended the funeral at Utter-McKinley's undertaking establishment on Sunset Boulevard and the interment of the ashes at the Hills of Home Mausoleum. He had seen the urn placed in a niche while an invisible organ piped "Ah, Sweet Mystery of Life" and all that was left of Max Vienna had been sealed, unmourned, in a marble wall. For Blayne, however, he still remained a living challenge, his suicide an unsolved puzzle.

At this point Simon Fennelley, in pink swimming trunks decorated with flamingos, appeared on the deck, waved, and made his way through the intervening tables grinning sheepishly. "How do you like my new drawers?" he wanted to know.

"Too bad Sergeant Lehny can't see you."

"Undignified?" Fennelley beckoned to a Filipino waiter and ordered two Zombies.

"Where's Moira?" Neddy asked.

"Went to her room to change."

"How did it go?"

"Very fast. No trouble." Fennelley stretched out thankfully in a lounge chair and squinted his eyes against the sun. "It's all wrapped up at this end."

"You won't go back right away, will you?"

He turned to Blayne. "Can you think of any reason not to?"

"A murder..." Neddy said idly, but he was thinking fast. "Suppose you discovered Max Vienna did not commit suicide? You might dig up some fresh evidence."

"We'd have to dig him up to prove it."

"Cremation," Neddy complained, "is so final. What plane will you take?"

"I might stay for the week end." The tall frosted-amber Zombies arrived and Fennelley payed for them. "My ulcer likes California," he pulled thirstily on the straws, "except for the traffic. It took us two and a half hours to get here from the Hall of Justice."

"I was in downtown Los Angeles once," Blayne said.

The policeman was pensive. "Now, if they had a subway..."

"Thinking of moving out?"

Fennelley denied it.

"All Easterners talk that way before they buy a house and set-tle down to commute with a Cadillac." Being a confirmed New Yorker, Blayne dismissed the subject. "Did they question Moira?"

"Very briefly. She told the same story."

"I know the story." Blayne recited it like a memory exercise. "She awakened in the middle of the night, discovered he was not in the house, ran out on the beach and found him with a gun in his hand. She tried to stop him but failed."

"Check." Fennelley was watching the other guests, tanned and carefree. If he resigned... A real-estate subdivision office floated into view, a desk with his feet on it, an orange grove out-side the open door, bees buzzing in the sun...

"Why wasn't she wearing her nightgown?"

"Because she thought he might be in the water."

"Let me try it again." Blayne spoke slowly, testing each word. "She awakened from a sound sleep, searched the house for him, remembered his preoccupation with suicide, and went back to her room for a bathing suit. No, I can't see it."

"Look, Neddy, maybe you wouldn't write it that way, but that's the way it happened. The coroner had to break his hand to remove that gun. No one could have shot him and put it there. Physically it's impossible."

"I agree with you—and yet, the impossible has happened before."

The younger man's attention was centered on a fishing boat anchored off the shore.

"It's difficult for me to believe Max Vienna would take his own life. Unless—" Blayne tapped his friend on the arm, realizing that he had lost his audience.

"Is this a new wrinkle on catathymic crisis, chum?"

"I was going to suggest a suicide pact."

"Me and you? This is so sudden, Neddy." The new Fennelley, who had just made a down payment on a fishing boat and was through forever with violent death, suddenly guffawed. "Max might have wanted to take her with him, but if I know Ryan, she wouldn't buy it."

"Maybe she had no choice," Neddy pointed out, "if he planned to kill her first."

"You're forgetting the highway patrolman. He heard Moira screaming and ran toward the sound. When he found them, Max Vienna was still breathing and the gun was clutched—" Fennelley's argument came to an abrupt halt, his eyes fixed on a face two tables away. "I think I know that girl." Vague memories stirred in Simon.

"California had done something to you, dear boy. Flamingos, and now women." The writer was curious, as always. "Which girl? The one with the hair?"

"No, the one with the cheekbones."

Neddy was instantly bored. "Oh, that one."

"She looks familiar."

"Doubtless. Her name is Candace Carstairs."

The Lieutenant gulped. "Good God, you mean the movie actress?"

"I believe she is one of our Duses of the Double Feature. You've heard of her?" he asked with intentional innocence.

"I used to keep a scrapbook about her." Fennelley was lost in admiration.

Neddy sat up straight. "That woman," he said in venomous tones, "wants to ruin my life."

Shocked, her admirer wanted to know how.

"I am referring to an autobiographical novel of mine. She wants to make 'Time's Fool' into a picture—an epic, I believe, was the word—like 'The Jolson Story.'"

"You know her?" Fennelley asked with new reverence. "I don't suppose you'd introduce me?" The former detective, who now owned a fleet of fishing boats, got to his feet in anticipation.

"The man on her right, wearing the zinc-oxide nose, is Jerome Lustig, her husband."

"Oh." Fennelley's ulcer showed its disappointment by a short jab to the midriff, and he sat down. "Here comes the Ryan."

In a black jersey Schiaparelli off-the-shoulder sweater, a black-and-white striped skirt, and thong sandals, Moira was a new person. Her hair, blonde again with bangs, was combed straight and just covered her ear lobes. Blayne watched her come toward them, Fennelley's last remark echoing in his ears—and an idea was born.

After she was seated, her cigarette lighted, three Zombies ordered, and greetings exchanged, Neddy made an excuse to draw Simon aside. "I'm afraid I rather lost my temper earlier this afternoon. I was supposed to have cocktails with them." He pointed with one eyebrow at Lustig's table. "I'm going to introduce you." Neddy steered his friend by the elbow. "Keep them talking. I don't care how you do it, but keep them here."

When Neddy rejoined Moira, he complimented her on her costume. "You look divine, darling."

"I do have some clothes," she said. "But that's all."

"You look quite different."

"I am. You see—" Moira was silent for a moment while the breakers crashed on the beach and the afternoon sun shone down on the white tables and the breeze fluttered their umbrella. "I fell in love with him."

"After ten years?"

"I began to know him." Her eyes appealed to Blayne, asking him to stop.

"We all forget, Moira. You don't think so now, but you will." He patted her hand. "Time—"

"Yes, I've heard that one," she said in a desperate social voice.

"Of course, I can't convince Fennelley now," the writer-criminologist went on blandly, "but I'm sure of my facts on catathymic crisis. Usually the original aggressive act serves as an antidote to greater mental disorganization. Did he seem normal to you?"

"He knew what he was doing," she answered quietly. The other people around them were chatting cheerfully about Palm Springs, dog trainers, and reducing diets. The new girl with bangs and bare shoulders spoke again. "How am I going to live, Neddy? What will become of me? How can I take care of Ronnie?"

He toyed with the straws in his glass. "You'll get vaudeville offers, naturally, and Sunday supplement—" Neddy stopped as if he had just thought of it. "Why don't you put the whole thing in a book?"

Moira's face brightened. "Do you think I could sell it?"

"I'll sell it for you—to that gentleman over there. He's a producer."

"Movies?"

"Mm. I think he's waiting to talk to me. I refused an offer he made."

Moira wasn't interested in Blayne's problem. "How much could I get?"

"Oh, that depends."

"On what?"

"How good it is, who wrote it—a great many other things. What your collaborator would want."

"Oh, no," she said casually. "I'd write it myself." But after a reflective pause, a little frown creased her brow. "Where would I start?"

"That's always important. And where to stop."

"I don't see how I could explain Max's life without going back and—"

"Yes?"

"Those last hours—he told me things no one would believe unless—"

"That will come in the writing."

"Will it?" Her enthusiasm faltered. "I suppose I could take one of those courses. Is there a lot to it?"

"A few tricks," he said.

"If I could only tell someone—talk it, don't you know, to someone who could write it down." She leaned toward Blayne like an earnest sophomore. "Would that be collaborating?"

The greatest living playwright nodded.

Moira held out her hand almost boyishly. "Could we split—fifty-fifty?"

Blayne did not take her hand.

"What would you want?" she asked, a little hurt.

"Nothing."

She brightened. "You'd write it for nothing?"

"My dear, a real artist does not collaborate with anyone but himself and God."

Moira Ryan knew how to take a brush-off. "You shouldn't have led me on, Neddy. That was rather naughty of you."

"I'll probably write my own version," he replied casually. "But don't worry, darling, you won't recognize yourself." Then, closing his eyes, he waited a beat. "Of course, I'll change the ending. It's all wrong. For a play, there must be a neat curtain, a little twist. Yes, I think I'll have *her* kill *him*."

Moira looked at him steadily. "How?"

"I've no idea yet. How would you suggest?"

"I'm a slow study, darling." She held his eyes. "Sorry it took me so long."

"My curiosity will be the death of me." Neddy gave her a wan Baudelairian smile.

"It could easily be."

"Once you've killed someone, they say you have no further qualms about bloodshed." Neddy discovered that he was suddenly very cold. "I wonder if that's true."

"No qualms," said Moira, "and no scruples. I think."

"Lustig offered me a hundred thousand for 'Time's Fool.' I'll get the same price for you—and write the script myself. Agreed?"

"A hundred for me? That's an awfully important figure."

"So am I."

"All of it?"

"Absolutely."

"What would I do for that?"

"You don't have to do anything—but supply the ending."

This time Blayne offered his hand. "Would you like to think it over? I'm really doing this for Ronnie. You can trust me."

"I trust you, Neddy dear, but don't bring Ronnie into it. You're offering me a hundred grand on one condition—that I satisfy your curiosity." And then she told him.

Sebastian Blayne was smiling when he stopped at Jerome Lustig's table. "Don't get up. Please." Fennelley was eating spare ribs with sweet-and-sour sauce, hot egg rolls, and fried shrimp without taking his eyes off Candace. "You have been very patient. Thank you for waiting."

"Were we waiting?" Candace hadn't realized it. Her first principle was to keep others waiting. "Simon has been so entertaining."

"You have changed your mind, I hope?" the producer asked.

"Yes, Mr. Lustig. We'll change the title and the plot a teeny bit, but I'll do the script."

"What about my part?" the actress asked.

"It's your picture, darling. You were quite right."

"Definitely."

Lustig smelled a rat. "The writer is still in it?"

"Oh, yes, I'm in it. But now I think we should celebrate. I'd like you to meet my friend—if we may join you?"

Fennelley had never seen Blayne so polite. He also smelled a rat.

A moment later Neddy returned with Moira in tow and made the introductions.

"This is Mrs. Hadley, a fellow artist and writer from New York."

Fennelley dropped a spare rib.

Candace was charmed.

Lustig was delighted. "But haven't we met before? I know your face. I never forget a face."

Before the producer could remember, Neddy said, "I've been discussing the picture with Mrs. Hadley and she's come up with a splendid idea." He turned to Fennelley and signaled for co-operation. "I hope this won't bore you, Simon."

And without more ado Neddy began to outline the story.

"...after which Candace invites the writer for cocktails, and while he is there—this scene has a rather amusing pay-off with the dog—the murderer enters the apartment and returns her mink coat. She somehow senses her lover's presence and is terrified. Because, you see, Candace knows—part of her mind has always known—that he—shall we call him Paul?—that Paul intends to kill her."

"I don't believe it," Lustig said. "But I'll ask my psychiatrist."

"You should have your head examined, sweetheart," the wife replied. "We all know things subconsciously without admitting we do. Like sex." She smiled at Fennelley. "Isn't that right?"

Neddy protested the interruption and continued. For half an hour he talked as only Sebastian Blayne could when he chose, spinning an intricate web of illusion, clothing the characters with flesh, putting blood in them_ and tears. He conjured up empty rooms and furnished them with his inspiration. And before their eyes the puppet that was Paul became a person who walked and talked like Max, knew fear and lust, felt pain, inflicted pain, and suffered an agony of confusion, as Blayne created something more than the truth, something other than the tawdry tragedy of Ida, something beyond the lives of Max and Moira, fabricating what he did not know, inventing the neatly revealing touch, and holding his audience with the old, old magic of the storyteller.

"And so, that night after their gay and ghastly party, he asks her to go swimming. It is a dark night—no moon—a storm blowing up. Can you hear the music behind this scene as they go down the beach to the cove? There he makes love to her."

"Bad motivation. She wouldn't let him touch her at a time like that," Lustig muttered.

"Oh, yes, she likes it. She wants him." The actress understood. "She's still horribly attracted to him, even though she knows he means to kill her."

"You mean this fellow hasn't tipped her when he's going to do it or how?" Fennelley wanted to know.

"That's good suspense." Lustig approved. "And then?"

"While she's lying in his arms Candace feels the gun in the pocket of his robe."

"I'm able to steal it?" Her gaunt eyes were burning.

"No. You have a better idea. Safer. You remember something Paul has mentioned, in connection with the murder in Jamaica. And you make him tell you this story again, teasing him to describe the girl and what he did to her. Paul becomes very excited, reliving the whole thing. In his madness, or his recollection of it, you become the girl, and his arm aches as he remembers. You're hypnotizing him, really—weaving a spell, forcing him back to that time, making him paralyze his arm again, detach it, lose control of it."

"Oh, I can see it!" The girl's thin face was glowing with an inner fire that millions worshiped. "It's a wonderful scene for me. I do this Svengali thing and give him the gun—"

"Of course. And all the while you're whispering to him and caressing him, stroking his arm and hand, testing it to find out. Finally you dig your nails into his flesh, and kiss him once more, passionately, before you put your hand over his and pull the trigger."

Lustig sat back and let out his breath. "Terrific. But I don't know. Do you think we could make it believable?"

Fennelley got up and stretched. "I believe it," and with a slight bow in Neddy's direction added, "I think you can get away with it, Blayne. You'll probably lose sympathy for Candace, but, after all, it *was* self-defense."

Lustig turned to Moira. "What about you, Mrs. Hadley? Do you believe a woman could be capable of such a thing?"

"But the trick with the gun was Mrs. Hadley's idea," Blayne protested. "You can't ask *her*."

And that is how I happened to write this book.

ABOUT THE AUTHOR

Jan Huckins was born in 1911 in Oklahoma City, where her parents owned the Huckins Hotel (her mother later jumped to her death from the 8th floor in 1949). She wrote freelance articles for newspapers and magazines and ghost-wrote the scripts (for writer Irma Phillips) for the popular 1942 radio serial *Lonely Woman*, which she also novelized. Under the pen name "Sebastian Blayne," she wrote two private eye novels, *Holiday in Hell* (aka *Ghastly Holiday*) and *Terror in the Night* in the early 1950s. Huckins died in Santa Monica, California in 1981.

www.ingramcontent.com/pod-product-compliance
Lightning Source LLC
Chambersburg PA
CBHW030256270626
47156CB00022B/2776